SIN
The Seventh Day
By Leslie Swartz

Copyright 2020, Leslie Swartz

Library of Congress Control Number: 2020925850

ISBN: 9798587473843

Either thou or I, or both, must go with him.

Romeo and Juliet, Act 3, Scene 1

Prologue

Twenty-two-year-old Wyatt slumped in his seat on the sofa in Clear View's rec room, the combination of Risperidone and Lithium making him lethargic. As tired as he felt, he couldn't sleep. His hallucinations had always been bad but since arriving at the upstate mental hospital, they had grown in frequency and intensity. What used to be sporadic was now constant with not one figment of his imagination but several, and all the time. Even now, heavily medicated and half-conscious, he saw a man staring out the caged window, his robe slightly opened, a bit of drool dribbling from his dry, parted lips. The man didn't seem to be aware of his surroundings, but why would he be? He wasn't real, just like the woman twirling in front of the television and the teenager that paced the floor mumbling obscenities.

"Come on, asshole," Wyatt whispered to himself. "Get it together. They're not real."

"Excuse me?" an orderly asked, leaving his post at the door and walking toward him.

"Nothing, I'm just talking to myself." Wyatt hung his head and muttered, "What else is new?"

"Really? Because it sounded like you called me an asshole. Did you just call me an asshole?"

"What? No. I was--"

"Because I don't think it would be in your best interest to insult me, do you?"

Wyatt lifted his head, his steely eyes boring into the would-be bully. Through gritted teeth, he tried to defuse the situation, knowing the consequences of having an outburst in a place like this. "I wasn't speaking to you."

"Are you giving me attitude?" He bent down, his face now only inches from Wyatt's. "Because it sounds like you're giving me an attitude."

He trembled with rage as he tried to control his emotions and remain seated. Every part of him wanted to rip the man to shreds. It took everything in him to stay still as he gripped the edge of the couch cushion and clenched his jaw. "I'm not."

"That sounds like backtalk to me." The orderly stood and cracked his neck. "Maybe you need a lesson in manners. What is it you're here for? Hallucinations? What do you think, bitch? Am I real or something your fucked up brain invented?"

Wyatt seethed as the orderly laughed.

"See, I think you have no idea what's real and what's in your head. You don't even know if *you're* real, do you?"

Wyatt bit his lip so hard he drew blood as the fatigue he'd been feeling was replaced with a surge of adrenaline. His heart pounded in his chest as his breathing quickened. His knuckles went white as his fingers dug holes in the sofa's pleather seat.

"Is Wyatt even your name? Maybe you're not even here. Maybe--"

But, before he could finish, Wyatt was on his feet, hurling himself into the man and knocking him to the ground. He sat on his chest and punched him, first in the eye and then breaking his nose. Blood splattered as he continued his assault, the other patients screaming and cowering in corners. Two more orderlies came to their coworker's rescue, prying Wyatt off of him and dragging him away. He fought them, pushing and punching. One got him in a choke-hold, but Wyatt grabbed his arm and raised it to his mouth, biting down on the man's flesh causing him to scream in pain.

A nurse rushed over, tapping the glass of a syringe as she got close.

Wyatt grunted as the first orderly got to his feet, aiding the others in restraining him. "No," he demanded. "No more drugs." But, her compassionless eyes never even looked at his face. She rubbed a spot on his arm with alcohol and administered the injection. Almost immediately, he felt weak, his legs giving out underneath him. He did his best to struggle as the men dragged him to his room, but it was no use. He was fading fast and as they strapped him to the bed, he didn't even feel it as the first man punched him in the stomach and diaphragm.

The others left the room while the first orderly spat on him, landing one more blow to his abdomen before turning the light off and closing the door as he left. Just when he thought things couldn't get much worse, the woman's voice was back. It had been a few days since he'd heard it, but now it was clear as day, ringing in his head as loud as ever.

Tell me where you are. She sounded upset, almost like she was crying. *I can't help you if you don't tell me. Answer me, please.*

His eyes rolled back as the medicine worked its magic. *At least I'll finally get some sleep*, he thought, his eyes closing, the world and the woman's voice fading into oblivion.

Chapter 1

Sinclair dragged the toes of her shoes through the bits of tire that cushioned the ground under the swing as she sat, head resting on the chain as she watched the children with their parents playing happily on the other side of the park. She didn't avert her glance when Gabriel approached and sat next to her or when she pulled a candy bar from her bag and handed it to her.

"Thanks," the girl said, eyes still on the family of strangers as she peeled open the wrapper and took a bite.

"Your mother's worried sick," Gabriel said, taking a bite of her own candy bar and following her niece's stare.

"Which one?"

"Uriel. Michelle's so busy trying to make your first birthday party perfect, she doesn't even know you're gone."

"I'm thirteen."

"Not according to the calendar."

"You know what I mean."

"Yeah, I do."

She took another bite and swallowed before speaking again, glancing over to her aunt who finished her candy and put the wrapper in her bag. "She's going to a lot of trouble?"

"She's making a cake from scratch. Her skills in the kitchen are almost as bad as mine. I don't have high hopes of it being edible. Girl's lucky she met your dad. Without him feeding her decent meals, she'd eat...well, like I do."

"So, effort, is what you're saying."

She met her niece's gaze, the pain in her expression breaking her heart. "She wants it to be special for you. She starts school soon and she's having some anxiety about being away from you for that many hours a day. And she feels guilty."

"She doesn't need to."

"I told her, but what do *I* know?"

She laughed, taking one last bite of candy and giving the wrapper to her aunt who put it in her purse. She again looked to the family across the park and held on to the swing's chains, resting her head on the warm metal. "I'm getting too old for this, aren't I?"

Gabriel's heart was heavy as she patted the girl's back.

"Okay. You can take me home now."

Gabriel gripped the chains of her own swing. "We can stay a little longer." She kicked her feet out and swung back and forth, a tiny smile forming on Sinclair's lips as she, too, began to swing.

Michelle peeked through the window in the oven to see the cake had finally risen. She breathed a sigh of relief as she checked the timer and scurried back to the dining room to begin filling purple and white balloons with helium. Clusters of twinkle lights hung from every inch of the ceiling and streamers papered the walls so completely, not a speck of paint showed through. The party was taking shape and she couldn't wait to see her daughter's reaction to the room's transformation.

As she fiddled with the rented helium tank, she heard the front door slam. She went to investigate, seeing Sinclair bolting up the stairs and heading to her room.

"Thanks for bringing her home," Valerie told Gabriel as they stood in the entry. "I about had a heart attack."

"Where was she?" Michelle asked, worry covering her face as she approached.

"Just at the park again," Gabriel said.

Valerie crossed her arms and shook her head. "This is the third time this month that girl has run off."

Michelle leaned on the banister and rolled her eyes. "She's just going down the street to the park. She's thirteen, not three."

Valerie smacked her lips. "You weren't here when that Baba whatever-the-hell attacked her. I still have nightmares about it. I don't want her going out alone. Who knows what other monsters might be waiting to--"

"She's fine," Gabriel interrupted. "She's not five anymore. If something tried fucking with her *now*, God help them."

Valerie bit her bottom lip, casting an annoyed glare at her sister. "Why you always gotta undermine me?"

"I just don't want you to worry for no reason."

"I have *every* reason."

Gabriel saw the memories flashing in Valerie's mind, the beatings doled out by various abusive foster parents, the bullies at school, and the time spent alone, neglected for days on end, sometimes with no food. Her features softened as she placed a hand on her sister's shoulder. "Sinclair isn't you and *you* are *not* the people that raised you. You're a good mother. Believe me, I would tell you if you weren't."

She laughed.

"She just needs a little time alone. Okay, I have to go. Wendy's moving in today and I promised I'd help her unpack."

Valerie raised her eyebrows. "Moving in? That's a big step for you, seein' as how up until you met her, you were handing your ass out like Halloween candy."

"Hey," She held a finger up in protest, then dropped it. "All right, that's valid."

Valerie walked Gabriel to her car leaving Michelle to look up to the second floor, too impatient to give her daughter the space Gabriel said she needed. She hurried up the steps and knocked on Sinclair's door before opening it.

"Can I come in?"

The girl shrugged.

She slipped into the room, closing the door behind her. Sinclair was at the chalkboard, furiously drawing something Michelle couldn't make out. It was a sea of orange, red, and gray with no real shape to it. She sat on the bed and watched, the cold determination on the girl's face unnerving. "Are you okay?"

"As okay as ever," she answered, her eyes fixed on her work.

"You freaked Valerie out leaving like that."

"I didn't mean to."

"I know. She's just being overprotective. Maybe let one of us know before you head out next time."

She stopped what she was doing, glanced over to her mother, and nodded.

"You sure you're okay?"

Sinclair relaxed her shoulders and looked around the room. "This used to be Gabriel's room when she was a kid. I feel sad for her. Some really bad things happened to her in this house."

"Like what?"

"Just parent stuff."

"Oh. Well, you don't have to worry about Gabriel. She turned out fine. No matter what life throws at her, she catches it and makes it her bitch." She covered her mouth. "I'm so sorry. Don't repeat that word in front of Valerie. She'll give me a lecture and I don't need her telling me how to parent one more time today."

She smiled. "You know I've heard her say way worse, right?"

"Yeah. I suspect she beats *herself* up over it, too. So, is that what's been bothering you? Gabriel told you some horror story from her childhood and it's put you in a mood?"

She sighed heavily, looking up as if in deep thought as she put the chalk down. She brushed the residue from her hands and sat next to her mother. "Do you think she's happy?"

"Well, she's moving in with her girlfriend, so probably."

"Yeah. Mom,"

"What, baby?"

"Are you happy?"

She smiled and put her hand on her knee. "Yeah, baby, I'm happy. Why wouldn't I be?"

"Gabriel said you feel guilty about school."

She clicked her tongue. "Your aunt should really mind her business sometimes."

"I don't want you to feel bad about--"

"I'm all right. Mom guilt is a totally normal thing. I know logically that you're growing up and you don't need me as much. I've put off school long enough. It's time to get my crap together. But, I feel bad about being gone a lot, just like any mom with a job does. It's nothing for you to worry about, okay?"

She nodded.

"Okay," She kissed her head and stood. "Now, stay out of the dining room for a while. It's not ready, yet."

"Okay, Mom."

She left the room, Sinclair's cold gaze returning to the chalkboard. She went back to it, picking up the orange chalk, and beginning again.

Chapter 2

"What do you think?" Will asked as he and Malik stood in the center of the empty room that looked more like a warehouse than an office building.

Malik glanced around at the exposed beams and ductwork, the studs, and the huge window at the front of the building. "It's big. What are you gonna do with it?"

"I'm converting it to a restaurant."

"Oh, congrats. You've certainly got the space for it here."

"Yeah," Will crossed his arms. "It's just," He paused.

"Just what?"

"I mean, don't get me wrong, cooking's great. But, if I'm being honest, it's just a hobby for me. I don't love it the way you do."

"Most people don't," he winked.

"Do you want it?"

"Want what?"

"The restaurant."

Malik stepped back. "Boy, you trippin'. I'm not about to work for *you*."

He laughed. "I don't want you to work for me. This would be *your* place. I'd just be an investor."

"I appreciate you thinking of me, kid, but I don't need any favors."

"Who's doing you a favor? I've been eating your food for months. I know how good you are. You could make us both a *ton* of money."

"I don't know, man. Getting into business with family? What if it fails?"

Will shrugged. "Then, I just rent the space to someone else. No harm done."

He chuckled. "That's cold."

"All the apartments are rented. I have an on-site handyman and an office next door where I basically sit and count my money all day. I'm bored. I need a project but I don't want to run a restaurant. *You* do."

He looked around again and rubbed his chin.

"And, who knows? If this place does well, maybe I open more restaurants around town."

"Well, look at you, four years old and already a mogul."

He gave him an exasperated glare. "That joke's getting really old."

"Maybe, but you're not."

"Are you in, or what?"

Malik sighed. "Why not?"

"Awesome." They shook hands, both men smiling. "Let's get to work."

"All right, Pearl," Wendy said, placing the terrarium on top of the dresser and turning on the red UVA light. "We're not just staying the night this time. We live here now. I know it'll be an adjustment for you, but you'll get used to it. You like Gabriel, right?"

"You're talking to the lizard?" Gabriel asked, sauntering into the room and sitting on the bed.

"She's a snow leopard gecko, thank you, and yes, I'm talking to her. This is a big move for her. She needs reassuring."

"*She* does, or *you* do?"

Wendy turned, a playful smirk curling her lips. "I'm fine. I've never lived with anyone, so it's a little weird, but a good weird." She sat, brushing the long, dark hair off her girlfriend's shoulder. "First day of summer vacation weird. Pearl, though, will have to get used to being in a new environment. Hopefully, feeling how calm I am settles her nerves."

"If you say so." Gabriel ran a hand over Wendy's thigh. "Far be it from me to question the communication between a witch and her familiar."

She touched her cheek and went in for a kiss, but before their lips could meet, her phone buzzed in her pocket. She pulled it out and read the text. "It's Lucifer. He's in Tristan da Cunha. Pretty." She turned the screen so Gabriel could see the picture he'd sent of the remote island from above.

"That's super interesting. So, you were saying?" She leaned in but the phone buzzed again.

"He says he's running out of quiet places to think."

She rolled her eyes. "How sad for him."

"He says he's even starting to miss you."

"For Christ's sake." She stood and took her own phone from her back pocket, texting to her brother, *I miss you, too, but I need you to stop texting my girl now. It's moving day and I'm tryna christen this new mattress.*

"What did you say?"

"I said I miss him, too."

Her phone buzzed again and as she read the text, she couldn't help but laugh. "He says, 'Apparently, I've interrupted something tawdry. I'll speak to you later'."

"Okay, phones up." She took both cells and dropped them in the nightstand's drawer before crawling across the bed to Wendy on the other side. She kissed her delicately before pulling her top off. "I hope Pearl's not shy because there's about to be a show."

As the two kissed again, removing each other's clothes, the gecko scurried in her habitat, drinking from her bowl, and hiding in her ceramic cave. The phone buzzed again, but this time, the women were too preoccupied to notice.

Lucifer laughed as he put his phone away, taking in the ocean view, the water so blue, it almost made him forget how unhappy he was. He was still, after all his time, unable to settle his conscience. Racked with guilt and shame, feeling that every day he remained on Earth was another day he failed as a son, he wandered, searching for meaning in his now directionless existence. He wished that he could enjoy his time on Earth, knowing that in just over two hundred years, his Father would wake and send him back to the depths, either as Watch Keeper or as a new inmate. But, there was no joy to be had. He'd disobeyed, putting human lives before his duty. He'd defied God's command and he knew better than anyone that there was no coming back from that.

Wyatt looked over his notes as the instructor drew a cross-section of a heart on the whiteboard. The man put the marker down and addressed the class of would-be paramedics. "So we've talked about STEMI, ST elevation, ST depression, and T rate inversion. Tomorrow, we'll be discussing cardiac axis and axis deviation. Think of the cardiac axis as the mean vector in which the electrical activity of the heart flows. So, you've got your SA node here," He picked the marker back up and wrote the letters 'SA' in the top left corner of the heart. "And you've got your intra--" He caught a glimpse of the clock on the back wall and stopped. "Hey, sorry, guys. I've kept you over again. We'll get back to this tomorrow. Have a great day."

Wyatt and the other students gathered their belongings and left the classroom. As he exited the community college, he found Allydia waiting for him, coffee and danish in hand.

"My hero," he said, taking the cup and gulping down the warm contents.

She took his books so he could eat as they walked. "You left without eating. It isn't healthy."

"I was running late."

"Learning to take care of others shouldn't interfere with taking care of yourself."

He swallowed a bite of danish. "It's sweet of you to worry about me, but I'm all right."

"All right isn't good enough for you. You deserve amazing."

"Aw, look at you caring about me," he teased.

"Are you sure this is what you want to be doing?"

"School? Yeah, why?"

"You've been tired."

"I'm just not used to getting up this early. It'll be fine once I get my schedule fixed."

They walked in silence for a while as he finished his breakfast. He tossed his trash in a bin as they approached the subway.

Allydia stopped at the entrance, touching his arm as she looked up at him. "I don't want you to think I disapprove."

"I don't."

"I think it's noble what you're doing. I'm very proud of you."

"Thank you, but I don't know if I'd call it 'noble'."

"It's training to save lives. What would *you* call it?"

"I don't know, it just feels like," He took the books and looked them over before returning her gaze. "What I'm supposed to do."

"There is no 'supposed to' in this life, Wyatt. There is only what you decide. You choose what you do and you have chosen kindness, service to others. There is nothing more noble than that."

He tucked her hair behind her ear. "I'm not sure if that's incredibly insightful or if you just love me."

She flashed a mischievous grin. "I'm fairly certain it's both."

He laughed and gave her a quick kiss before leading her to the subway. "Sometimes, I forget you've been collecting wisdom for thousands of years."

Chapter 3

Navid paced in the alley, hugging his arms as his patience wore thin. He'd been waiting for over an hour and he was beginning to think his informant wasn't going to show. Finally, a man scurried into the alley, hands trembling as he lit a cigarette. "You him?" he asked, blowing out a puff of menthol-laced smoke.

Navid nodded.

The man looked behind him, eyes wild.

"Were you followed?"

"I don't think so." He took another drag and set his eyes on Navid. "You can never be too careful with them Mare Boys, though, yeah?"

"That's facts. So, what've you got for me?"

"They just pulled a job in Hackney. Not sure what they nicked, but they filled a whole van with boxes. Must be important to 'em because even Duncan was there."

His ears perked up. "Duncan Laurence?"

"Who else, mate? Yeah, the big guy himself. He watched 'em load up the boxes, never gettin' *his* hands dirty, then they drove off. I followed them, just like you said. They're hole up in a warehouse near Olympic Park."

"Of course, they are."

"These bloke's ain't messin' round, yeah? You go in, you best be packin' because they will be."

"Don't worry about me, mate." He lifted his shirt to show off the Glock 17 in its belt holster. "I'm Flyin' Squad. I haven't been unarmed for six months."

The man took a step back. "That gun's real serious."

"Yeah, well," Navid put his shirt back down. "So am I."

15

Navid sleuthed in through a broken window of the long-abandoned warehouse, scanning the room as he positioned himself behind a tower of pallets. There were five men, all in jeans and tee-shirts unloading crate after crate from a windowless van. A sixth man wearing dark slacks and a brightly-colored flower-print button-down took stock of a crate's contents as it was placed before him, writing on a legal pad and nodding for another to be opened when he was finished.

"Duncan," Navid muttered as he took out his phone and quickly snapped several pictures of the van's license plate, the men's faces, and the crates which, with the help of his phone's zoom, he could see were full of watches, each worth at least twenty-four thousand pounds retail. With his zoom he could also see that the men all carried pistols, the jeans-wearers' shoved down the back of their pants, and the flower-shirted man sporting a shoulder holster.

In the distance, he could hear water dripping. Not surprising given the condition of the building. There were probably leaks everywhere. But, it hadn't rained in days. As he took one last picture of the side of the van, he noticed a small puddle seeping out from underneath it. It was leaking oil at a rapid rate. If they gave chase, that would make it easier to follow or track them. "Good to know," the detective whispered to himself.

"Is someone there?" Duncan called. The others pulled their guns and pointed them in the direction their leader was looking.

Navid held his breath for a second. He'd spent the last several months gathering information on this gang and Duncan Laurence in particular. He knew his address, his daily routine, even the name of his favorite actress. He knew his associates, his relatives, and his barber. He knew he hated olives, liked bacon more than anyone he'd ever met, and had a soft spot for beagles. He knew he'd had a vasectomy in his twenties and had come to regret it when, just last week, his wife filed for divorce on the grounds of fraud. Apparently, he'd never disclosed that bit of information. Navid had been surveilling the head of the Mare Boys for months but he'd never been able to catch him in any wrongdoing. This was the break he needed. He couldn't let it slip through his fingers.

"Oi!" Duncan called again. "Who's there?" He set his paper and pen on the crate in front of him and walked around it, stomping toward what he could now see was a man sitting on the dirty cement leaned up against a stack of pallets. He waved his hand, signaling the others to put their guns down. The man was passed out, phone in hand, mouth hanging open. Duncan kicked his leg, waking the man and laughing. "He's sloshed!"

The others chuckled as they threw tarps over their ill-gotten gains, hiding them from the drunk stranger.

Navid squinted up at him, slurring his words. "You're not Penelope."

"No, mate. You're in the wrong spot. Do you know who I am?"

Navid shook his head.

"Good. That's real good. Do you know any of my friends?"

He glanced around the corner of the pallets and back up at him, shaking his head again.

"Brilliant. And, do you know what we're doin' here?"

Navid feigned sleepiness as he stood, catching himself on the pallets as he pretended to be dizzy. "Looks like," He pointed to a rusted-out forklift. "Workin'?"

"You could say that, yeah. And, what exactly are *you* doin' here?" He snatched the phone and opened the picture file. His eyebrows raised and his lips curled into a sickening grin. "Well, well, well. I see why you were disappointed that I wasn't Penelope." He turned the screen to show the others the picture Gabriel had taken of herself all those months before. They whistled and whooped in approval as he turned the screen back, giving it another once-over. "She's *fit*. What are you doin' here? If I was you, the only way I'd get outta *her* bed is in a body bag."

Navid grabbed the phone and shoved it in his pocket. "That's a bit disrespectful, innit?"

"Probably, yeah. But, you know what else is disrespectful? Stumblin' into *my* place, sozzled, knackered, and uninvited."

"Good thing I'm stone-cold sober, then," he said, his tone changed and his words clear. "Bright-eyed and bushy-tailed. And, I've got a warrant, so, no invitation needed." He winked before punching him in the nose and swiping the gun from the gang leader's holster. He spun him around, Duncan holding his nose and wincing in pain. He held him to his chest while pointing the gun at the others. "All right, then. Down they go, nice and easy." The men traded ornery looks, snickering as they set their eyes on the detective and opened fire.

Duncan was shot in the leg, falling to the ground as Navid dropped him, diving behind the pallets of wood. They charged toward him, shooting haphazardly in his direction. He returned fire, hitting the two closest in the abdomens.

"Let's just go, man!" one of them shouted. The three still standing made a break for the van, two hopping in the back and shutting the doors while the last climbed in the driver's seat.

Navid pulled the trigger again, but the gun was out of bullets. He threw it to the floor and pulled out his own gun. As the van sped toward the exit, Navid pursed his lips, cracked his neck, and took one final shot. The bullet hit the leaking oil tank, exploding the van in a ball of fire and sending metal and glass flying. The detective ducked down, covering his head as the back of the pallet wall got singed.

Duncan dragged himself across the concrete, determined to make his escape.

"Not today, mate." Navid grabbed him by his injured leg and yanked him back, pinning his arms to his back and cuffing him.

"What the fuck, Navid?!" A woman's voice echoed from behind.

"Hey, Pen," he greeted. "Nice of you to join."

The female detective and a handful of bobbies stormed in. The officers checked the van for survivors, finding the driver with a head wound but still breathing.

"We don't just blow shit up, Navid. This isn't America."

He laughed, pulling Duncan up with him as he stood. An officer rushed over and dragged him off. "Have fun in prison, blank-shooter!"

"And, taunting a suspect?" she lectured. "I know you've been after this guy for a while, but--"

"I'm just havin' a bit of fun. I deserve it, yeah?"

She furrowed her brow and watched through the open doors as officers loaded the suspects into the Transit. "You do get results, I'll give you that."

He checked the time on his phone. "All right. I'll meet you at the station to get this paperwork squared away."

She tilted her head. "It's late. You should get some sleep. Paperwork can wait until morning."

"You know what they say. Why put off until tomorrow what can be done today?"

"See, this. This right here."

"What?"

She shook her head. "This is why we didn't last. You never stop workin'. You get four hours of sleep a night, if that, and when you're not doin' the job, you're wishin' you were."

"Lot's of criminals on the streets, Pen. And, if I'm rememberin' right, the reason we didn't work was because you was out shaggin' your ex while I was in hospital with a gunshot wound."

"It was a flesh wound and I didn't know you were hurt until after. Besides, I was only seein' him because I was unhappy with how things were between us. Your head was never out of the job, yeah? Doesn't matter. Point is, you're workin' too hard. Go home. Get some rest. Paperwork can wait."

"Yes, ma'am," he scoffed.

"I mean it. And, see about takin' some vacation time. It's not like you're not due. I say this with love, right? You need a break. Take a trip. Visit some family. Take care of yourself." She patted his arm and walked over to join the officers in examining the contents of the crates.

He sighed, not wanting to admit it to himself, but knowing she was right. "Family," he snorted. He looked down at his phone, pulling up his father's profile. He'd updated his cover photo with an image of him with yet another woman, laughing and holding glasses of red wine. "He does always seem to have a good time," he muttered to himself. Maybe visiting his long-lost dad wasn't the worst idea after all.

Chapter 4

"Excellent work, ladies," Phindi said as she wrapped up the class. "Before you go, what is rule number one?"

Twenty women responded in unison, "Anything to get away."

"Very good. I will see you all next week." She walked from her spot at the head of the room to the back where she had a display of items for sale. She stood behind the counter in case any of her self-defense students needed anything. As they filtered out, she eyed a woman who'd kept her sunglasses on the entire class. "Courtney," she called.

The woman jumped as she picked up her duffel bag. "Yes?"

"Come here, please."

She reluctantly made her way to the counter, adjusting her glasses to fit closer to her face. "Yes?"

She gestured toward her eyes. "Your sunglasses. Remove them, please."

"I-I'd rather not."

"I insist." Her tone was stern, her voice unwavering.

She slowly pulled the glasses down and off revealing a swollen and black left eye.

"As I suspected." She glanced around the room to make sure they were alone and pulled something out from underneath the counter.

Courtney examined the small metal object in her teacher's hand. "A barrette?"

"Not just a barrette. See here?" She pointed to its side. "A serrated edge. Wear it like this." She clipped it in the woman's hair just above her temple. "On the side of your dominant hand so it's easily accessible. When you are threatened and he is close, you simply pull it out and slash across the face, like this," She motioned over her own face to demonstrate. "Under one eye and across the bridge of the nose to the other side. Then, you run."

She swallowed hard, her eyes wide. "It works? It's so small."

"Just like you. Small but effective. I've watched you in class. You are capable of wielding much power. Strength does not come from size but from intention."

"How much?"

"There is no charge today. All I ask is that you make a promise, not to me but to yourself. If he does something like that to you again," She pointed to her eye as she slid her glasses back on. "You will leave and never return. You must remember, *pain* is not love."

She nodded. "Thank you."

The woman hurried out leaving Phindi to reflect on the conversation, one she'd had with at least a dozen women since she'd opened the gym to self-defense training. Sometimes, they came back the next week in better spirits, freed from their abusers. Other times, they didn't come back at all. She hoped to see Courtney again as she wondered what had happened to the ones that never returned.

Navid stood outside the museum, shifting his weight from one foot to the other as he tried to will his palms to stay dry. "What am I doing here?" he muttered to himself. "I must be one brick short." He shoved his hands into his pockets. "This was a mistake." He blew out a deep breath as he looked over the pale-blond sandstone and colonnaded pillars of the Neoclassical building. Everything in him was telling him to leave. His anxiety was through the roof. Gang members, murderers, bullets buzzing by his head, those he could handle without breaking a sweat. But, this, a meeting with his biological father was sending his heart racing.

Just as he was turning to go, he heard a voice from behind. "Navid?" He looked back. "It is you!" The older man with the light Italian accent rushed toward him, arms outstretched. He grabbed his shoulders and kissed both cheeks before taking his face in his hands as he looked him over. "Your photographs didn't do you justice! You're my spitting image! You have your mother's lips, though. You must get all the ladies, yes?"

"Not *all* of them," he said, a bit taken aback by his dad's warm reception. He'd only just sent him a message via social media that morning explaining who he was and asking if he had any interest in getting acquainted. He'd invited him for a visit immediately saying that he'd always wondered what had happened to his mother after their brief "romance". Navid had told him about his early years and that his mother had been killed so he was then adopted. His father had offered condolences and asked for pictures, which Navid sent.

Giovanni took a step back to get a better look at him. "I'm so glad you've come! You will stay with me, I insist. I'm having a party later tonight. Just a few friends. You must come."

"All right," Navid agreed.

He put his arm around his son and ushered him away from the building. "Have you been to Edinburgh before?"

"I have, actually."

"Wonderful, isn't it? Such interesting people. We should go to dinner. Have you tried Cullen skink? I know a fantastic place."

Navid smiled as they walked. Maybe he and his father had some things in common, after all.

They entered the Ramsay Garden flat, the geometric pattern of the coffered ceiling catching Navid's eye as he noticed the distinct tap his father's Italian leather loafers made on the old Scots Pine floors. Crystal chandeliers hung in the center of every room including an office nook off the living room with curved walls that couldn't have been more than a couple of feet wide. Tasteful burgundy Kashan rugs decorated the floors while shuttered windows and built-in cabinetry lined the walls.

"Nice place."

"Oh, thank you," Giovanni said, looking around the living room as if seeing it for the first time. "I kept it as true to its history as I could, with a few modern conveniences, of course."

He looked down the hall, the number of doors seeming excessive for a man living alone. "How many bedrooms?"

"Three. Mine is at the end of the hall, you can take the one on the left. It has its own en suite."

"Why so many, if you don't mind me askin'?"

"Well, one never knows when one might have guests." He winked as a knock came on the door. He answered it, letting in nine women, all beautiful and all salaciously dressed. "Welcome, ladies. This is my son, Navid. He's on vacation." A few seconds after he'd closed the door, another knock came, this one louder, more insistent. "Excuse me."

"Navid," one of the women said, standing inappropriately close to him. "That's a pretty name. Where are you from?"

"London," he replied, taking a step back, the pungency of her perfume tickling his throat.

"No, I mean where are you *really* from?"

He furrowed his brow. "I'm *really* from London. I was born there, right? So, that's where I'm from."

"Don't be racist, Isla," another woman said, giving her a gentle nudge. "Don't you hear the Cockney accent? He's as British as they come, he is." She tossed her auburn curls over her shoulder and smiled up at him. "So, you're on vacation? What do you do?"

"I'm a detective." He shifted his gaze to the front door where his father shook the hands of five men as they entered. He couldn't be sure from the distance, but it looked to him like they were slipping money into his hand.

The woman's eyes grew wide and her face fell. "A detective?"

"That's right." He returned her stare, confused by the change in her expression.

"Does your father know that?"

"Yeah, I mentioned it. Why?"

"No reason." She hurried off, joining the others as they mingled with the new party guests.

"Well, that's not suspicious at all." He approached his father who greeted him with a broad smile.

"Navid, my boy. Are you having a good time? The ladies to your liking?"

"Everythin's on the up and up here, yeah?"

"What do you mean?"

He watched as the woman called Isla guided a man by the tie to one of the guest rooms. "I'm pretty sure you know exactly what I mean."

"Fine," he laughed, lowering his voice. "They're prostitutes. Who cares? They've all been tested if that's what you're concerned with."

"It's not."

"Don't get all poliziotto on me. It's perfectly legal here as long as no pimps are involved and I assure you, they are all here of their own accord. Why do you think I moved to this country? For the food?" He scoffed. "What I wouldn't give for proper arancini. But, it's worth it, no?"

He cast him a judgemental glare. "I saw you take money from those men. Comes off real pimpy to me."

"Just a door fee," he smirked. "For the party. Recouping my wine cost, that's all."

"Right." He rolled his eyes.

"Don't be so stuffy, Navid. Have some fun. You're on vacation, after all." He patted his shoulder and walked off to chat up one of the women.

"I knew this was a bloody mistake," he sighed. As he turned to leave, a man in an expensive suit and gold cufflinks breezed by. He was tall with pale skin and jet-black hair, the left side of the front of his jacket puffed out like he carried something hefty in an inside pocket. He couldn't put his finger on it, but there was something off about him that made Navid's cop sense tingle. Navid went to his father, the women dispersing at the sight of him. He got Giovanni's attention and gestured to the strange man. "Who is that, then?"

"I don't know," he admitted. "I don't remember seeing him before."

"So, you don't know anything about him?"

He shook his head.

"But, you let him in your place?"

"He must have come with one of the others. My parties are exclusive. One must be invited."

"But, not by you personally?"

He let out an exasperated sigh. "Lighten up, Navid! It's a party! With your looks, you could have your pick of ladies. My treat. Enjoy yourself." He rejoined the party guests while Navid watched the stranger take two women into the room that was meant to be his. His eyes became slits as the door closed. Something wasn't right about the man in the fancy suit and he was determined to find out what.

Inside the bedroom, the two women giggled as they sat on their knees on the four-poster bed. The man looked them over as he took the scourge from his jacket pocket. "Take off your clothes," he ordered, dropping the whip to his side as it snapped with electricity. The women did as they were told, lying back on the pillows as he made his way toward them, a crooked grin spreading across his dry lips.

Chapter 5

"Make a wish," Michelle said as Sinclair drew in a deep breath.

"Make it a good one," Valerie added.

Sinclair blew out the single candle as her family applauded and sang 'Happy Birthday'. Michelle cut the cake and placed the pieces on purple paper plates, handing each one to Valerie who then set them in front of the guests.

Will scooped ice cream and set a bowl in front of his daughter, kissing her cheek. "Did you get everything you wanted?"

She offered a half-hearted smile. "I always do."

He laughed and passed out bowls while Gabriel, Wendy, Allydia, and Malik ate. Wyatt sat at the other end of the table watching his granddaughter's face. She was pensive, trying to appear fine in front of the others, but she didn't fool him. He recognized that look. It was the same face Will had made when he first learned what he was. She was worried and as she snuck away, the party guests chatting happily, seemingly unaware of the concern in her features, Wyatt sighed, following her to where she sat on the staircase.

"You wanna talk about it?" He sat next to her, tying the loose string of his work boot.

She looked down at her hands in her lap. "Not really."

"Okay." He sat quietly, pretending to check his phone for text messages. After a while, she lifted her head and laced her fingers.

"Grandpa?"

He put his phone back in his pocket. "Yeah, sweetie?"

"I'm really sorry."

"For what?"

Tears pooled in her eyes as she fought to maintain her composure.

"Hey," He put his arm around her. "What's wrong?"

She sniffed. "I'm afraid."

"Of what?"

Her face was sullen as she struggled to find the words. "Growing up."

"You're worried about your powers?"

She averted her eyes and wiped away a tear. "I don't want any of you to get hurt."

He kissed the side of her head. "We won't."

"How can you be sure?"

He lifted her chin, looking her in the eyes and wiping away the fresh tears that spilled down her cheeks, a reassuring smile spreading across his lips. "We're pretty scrappy."

She laughed.

"There you are," Michelle said as she walked through the living room and into the foyer. "Your ice cream's starting to melt."

"I'm coming." Sinclair went with her mother back to the dining room and as the two disappeared from sight, Wyatt's expression changed. His smile faded and worry filled his eyes.

He crept up the steps and snuck into the girl's bedroom. Sinclair had always expressed herself through her art. He thought he might find some clues as to why she was so distraught in one of her sketchbooks but as he opened the door, the picture on the chalkboard wall made his heart jump. It was vivid, fire and smoke leaping from the black, gray figures lining the bottom in what looked like a river of blood. Through the haze, he could see a neon billboard. He recognized it almost immediately.

"Wyatt?" Allydia called from the hall behind him. "I've been looking everywhere for you. What are you--" She stopped, standing just behind him in the doorway. "Well, that's ominous. What is it?"

He swallowed hard, unable to take his eyes off the grim scene. "Times Square."

While Malik showered, Valerie climbed into bed, exhausted and ready to get some much-needed rest. But, before her head hit the pillow, she was gripped by a strangely familiar vision.

The street was empty save a few abandoned cars as several inches of rain slowly drained away, the rushing of the water in the sewer underneath so loud, it nearly drowned out the car alarm blaring in the distance. The air was thick with the stench of sulfur as she began to hear them, a few at first then hundreds. "Holy shit," she whispered, recognizing the raptor-like screech from a vision she'd had years before. It grew in intensity as it drew closer...the sound of screaming demons.

The voices were thousands now, shaking the ground and rattling windows. She put her hands to her ears, frantically looking around to see where they were coming from, but she couldn't pinpoint a location. They were all around her, everywhere and nowhere, the twisted laughs of the damned booming through the night like jets hitting Mach ten. Water turned to blood running over Valerie's feet as fires erupted on the street.

Her sight was obstructed by thick smoke as the noise grew so intense, it made her teeth chatter. She began to choke as she squeezed her eyes closed, coughing as tears ran down her cheeks.

She gasped, sitting up in bed, her hand flying to her chest as she fought to catch her breath. "It's over," she whispered to herself. "You're okay."

From the hall, Sinclair watched, arms folded, chewing the inside of her cheek in the dark. She backed away and headed to her room, Valerie never knowing she'd been there at all.

Hey! Valerie thought to her sister.
Gabriel responded, *What up, fam?*
Lucifer closed the gate to Hell, right?
He did.
Where is he now?
An island in the south Atlantic.
Still on his bullshit?

Yeah, trying to find himself or some kind of purpose or whatever. Like, I get it, but this has gone on for too long, I feel.

So, he can't open the gate back up, right?

No.

Valerie bit her lip. *You sure?*

Totes. Are you okay? It's late and I was just drifting off.

I'm fine. Just curious. Night.

Night.

Had she just passed out and had a weird dream, or was this a true vision? If it was the latter, she needed to tell her sister asap, but with the gate closed, it was impossible. It must have been a dream. "You're just tired," she told herself. But, after decades of premonitions, she knew in her bones her vision was real. She closed her eyes, hugging her pillow as she fell asleep, too tired to fight it. *Tomorrow*, she thought. *I'll think about it tomorrow.*

Chapter 6

Navid waited in his father's flat until morning when the strange man left. He followed him to an antique shop in Grassmarket where he stayed hidden but within earshot, listening to the conversation between the raven-haired man and the shop girl.

"Excuse me, miss?" he asked, his voice low and raspy.

"Yes, sir, can I help you?" she replied, too-red lipstick covering her thin lips.

"I'm looking for the owner of this store. Last I heard, he was going by 'Cain Adamson'. Is he here?"

Her face fell. "Are you friends?"

"I wouldn't say *that*."

Her shoulders relaxed. "Oh, good. I mean, not *good*, but...Mr. Adamson went missing about a year ago." She went behind the counter and took a business card from the drawer. She held it out to him. "This is his lawyer. He's been handling the estate and the like."

He took the card and nodded before spinning on his heel and exiting the shop. When he was sure he was gone, Navid approached the counter, pulling up a photo he'd taken of his ancestor when he'd been spying on him the night he'd met Allydia. He flashed his badge, taking the girl by surprise.

"Have I done something wrong?"

"No," he said, showing her the screen. "I just have a question. Is this the man you call Cain Adamson?"

Her eyes widened with hope. "Yes, that's him. Have you found him?"

"Sorry, love," He put his phone back in his pocket. "Your boss is dead."

She went pale. "What?"

He took a brochure from the counter and wrote his number on it, sliding it across to her and gesturing toward the entrance. "If you see that man again, give me a call, yeah?"

She nodded, taking the paper and placing it in the drawer. "He didn't kill him, right? He was looking for him."

"No, he didn't. He's a person of interest in a different case. Could be dangerous. Can I get one of those cards you gave him?"

She nodded, taking one from the drawer and handing it to him. "He did seem like a sleekit bastard. If he'd shaken my hand, I'd have to count my fingers after. Felt a little like I might boak when he was close. Do you know who *did* kill Mr. Adamson?"

"Yeah, he's been taken care of, as well. You don't have to worry about him comin' round."

She put her hand to her heart and breathed a sigh of relief.

"I've got to get back to work. Have a nice day." He turned to go.

"You, too!" she called after him, checking out his backside as he walked. As he left, she took the pamphlet from the drawer and twirled her hair as she looked at what he'd written. "Navid." She glanced up to the door, seeing him hurry off after his suspect. He hadn't flirted with her, but he'd been working. Maybe she'd call him later, whether the pale man came back or not.

Navid caught up to the man at the lawyer's office where he stood outside the window, using a hearing aid to listen in on the conversation inside.

The man flashed a sleazy grin as the lawyer asked how he knew Mr. Adamson. "Oh, we go way back. We did business together once in the old country."

The lawyer looked the man over, a suspicious eyebrow raised. "And, what country is that?"

"It hardly matters now, does it? The venture ended when he discovered I needed payment that he couldn't provide. Well, not *couldn't*. It was well within his ability. He just refused on moral grounds. *Him*." He laughed. "As if his ethical standards are so high."

"Yes, well, unfortunately, he's been missing for a little over a year. With no next of kin that we know of, his accounts have been frozen. The estate pays out what's needed to maintain his business and property but otherwise--"

"No next of kin, are you sure?"

"None that we can verify. There *is* a girl in the US he granted access to. She's the last living person with a claim to his considerable assets. But," He stopped, realizing he shouldn't be giving the stranger this much information. Why was he?

He leaned in, hands folded on the desk between them. "But, what?"

"She, she," He couldn't stop himself from talking. "She's in a coma."

"Where?"

He began to sweat. "A hospital in New York."

"And, what is her name?"

His eyes bulged as he loosened his tie. "I, I shouldn't,"

His eyes became slits. "*Her name.*"

"Ta, Tamsen Flagler."

He smiled, standing and adjusting his suit jacket. "And, what do I need to do to get access to Cain's accounts?"

The lawyer's hands shook violently as he reached behind to open a file cabinet, taking out a document and filling in the names and dates. "She would have to sign this." He held out the paper.

"That's it?" He snatched it away and looked it over.

The lawyer nodded as he began to feel queasy.

"Thank you. That will be all." He left the office, Navid keeping behind a bush as he dropped the hearing aid back in his pocket and pulled out his phone. He hadn't yet found it necessary to tap into the money Allydia had given him but chartering a flight to the States to beat this man to where he was going seemed like reason enough. Once that was done, he called his grandmother. When no answer came, he left a message.

"Hey, Gran. I'm on my way to New York. Somethin's fishy. It involves your dad. I'll call you when I know more."

He picked up his things from his father's flat, Giovanni still passed out from the shenanigans of the night before. He left a note saying he had urgent business involving a case and they'd speak again shortly. He wasn't sure if he would actually ever see his father again. He wasn't his favorite person by any means. He was morally corrupt and engaged in thinly veiled illegal activity. On the other hand, he *was* his dad and if there was a way to have even a casual holidays-and-birthdays-only relationship with him, he'd regret it if he didn't try.

He left the building and got in the black taxi. As he headed to the airport, he tried calling Allydia again before realizing it was only five AM in New York. "Idiot," he whispered to himself.

"What's that?" the driver barked.

"Not you. I was talkin' to myself. Forgot about the time change."

"Ah."

He sat back in his seat and gazed out the window at the beautiful old buildings as they passed. He thought about the dinner he'd had with his father before the illicit party, how they'd talked and laughed.

"So," the driver asked. "You're leaving us, then? Going back to where you came from?"

"No. Somewhere else."

"Ah, well. You think you'll be back?"

He sighed. "Maybe...one day."

Chapter 7

"You're finally up," Valerie said as Sinclair lumbered into the kitchen wearing jeans and a tee-shirt that was clearly too big for her. "Are those Michelle's clothes?"

The girl rolled her eyes as she opened the door to the walk-in pantry. "She won't mind." She went inside and began eating, shoveling snack bars, pretzels, and cookies in her mouth, barely chewing before swallowing the massive amount of food.

Valerie followed her into the pantry and handed her a bottle of water. "Were you up late?"

"No, I just needed to rest. Big day." She inhaled a granola bar and took the water.

Valerie laughed. "You got plans?"

She chugged half the bottle and replaced the cap. "You should eat something."

"I had breakfast with everyone else while you were still asleep."

"Something else. You need your protein."

"Girl, what is with you lately? One minute you're condescending and jumping rope with my last nerve and the next you're worried about my eating habits. Everyone else is gone for the day. It's just you and me. Tell me what's going on with you."

She put the bottle on a shelf and bit her lip. "You know I love you, right? Even when I'm awful. It's not your fault. I'm just...feeling overwhelmed."

"I love you, too, baby." She hugged her. "Why are you feeling like that?"

She pulled away, holding back tears. "I don't want to upset you."

She smirked. "I've been through a lot worse than teen angst. I can handle it, I promise."

A tear ran down Sinclair's cheek. "I'm sorry."

"For what, baby?"

As she reached for her water, her hand grazed a jar of jam, knocking it off the shelf and sending it crashing to the floor. "Sorry."

"It's all right, I'll get it." Valerie knelt down to clean up the mess. She winced as a broken shard sliced through her thumb. "Son of a--" She looked up to see Sinclair staring down at her hand. Her eyes went black and as her breathing quickened, her teeth began to extend. Valerie's heart leaped to her throat as she jumped back.

The girl covered her mouth, her eyes returning to normal as Valerie's skin healed itself. She dropped her hand to her stomach as fresh tears formed. "I'm so sorry." She fled the pantry and made a beeline for the front door.

"It's okay, I understand!" Valerie called after her. She raced to catch up.

"I'll make it up to you. Everything."

"What are you talking about?"

"Tonight." And with that, she was gone, moving so fast, Valerie couldn't even see which direction she'd gone.

"Shit."

Valerie searched everywhere for her daughter. The park first and the woods beyond it, the beach, and both of her favorite museums. She was nowhere to be found. Valerie returned home and called Wyatt, leaving a message asking if he could come to help look for her. She didn't want to involve her sister if she didn't have to. She had overstepped one too many times when it came to Sinclair. Just because she knew what she was thinking didn't mean she knew what was best for her. Gabriel wasn't her mother, *she* was. So, even though she hated invading her daughter's privacy and she'd never snooped before, she *needed* to find her. Maybe there was something in her room that would give her a clue about where she would go. She opened the door and what she saw on the chalkboard made her stomach drop. The smoke, the fire...the bodies. It was so similar to her vision, there was no way it was a coincidence.

Begrudgingly, she contacted her sister. *Hey.*

Gabriel responded, *What's the haps?*

She sat on the bed, eyes still fixed on the picture. *I think we need to talk.*

Chapter 8

The man strolled into the hospital room, not noticing Navid standing a few feet away in the hall. He took the chart from the end of the bed and flipped through it before tossing it over his shoulder. Navid peered in and watched as the pale man removed the girl's feeding tube and whispered something in her ear.

Her eyes flew open as she gasped for air, beads of sweat forming at her temples. The monitor beeped rapidly as her heart rate spiked.

"Hello, Tamsen," the man cooed. "Don't be afraid. Everything's fine. *Remain calm.*"

Her breathing slowed to normal and the monitor's noise quieted to an even, rhythmic pace.

"Good. That's very good, Tamsen." He handed her the document and a pen. "Sign this now."

She did as she was told, unable to take her eyes off of his pupils which seemed to change shape as he stared back at her.

"Lovely. Thank you." He took the items and hurried off, leaving her confused and blowing past Navid who pretended to be checking his phone for messages.

Navid waited until the man got on the elevator and the doors closed before entering the room himself. "Are you all right, miss?" he asked as she sat up. She looked around the room, taking in her surroundings, and putting together what must have happened.

"I'm not sure. How long have I been here?"

"I don't know, miss. I'm not a doctor. Would you like me to fetch one?"

"Who are you?"

"I'm a detective." He flashed his badge. "I followed that man here from Edinburgh. Have you seen him before?"

She shook her head.

"How did you know Cain Adamson?"

"What do you mean, 'did'?"
"He's dead. Were you friends or--"
"That's not possible."
"I assure you, it is."

She tilted her head as she looked him over. "Who did you say you were?"

"I'm a detective from London. I've been following the man that--"

"How did Cain die?"
"He was murdered."
"Well, he'd have to be, wouldn't he? By who?"
"The killer's also dead, ma'am. You don't have to worry."
"Okay, but, is Cain *dead* dead or just dead for now?"

He furrowed his brow. "Miss, how did you know Cain?"
"I didn't. She did."
"Who?"
"It doesn't matter. She's gone now. They got rid of her."
"Who's gone?"
"You remind me of someone. Have we met?"
"No. Are you all right, love? Should I call for a doctor?"

She reached a hand out to touch his cheek. "So familiar."

He gently brushed her hand away. "Who knew Cain? Why did he give you access to all of his money?"

"She had ways of making him do what she wanted. He wouldn't have sex with her because he said I was too young, so she convinced him it was necessary. The money would pay for the army."

"You're not makin' any sense, love. Let me get you a doctor." He turned to go but she grasped his arm, the realization causing her to jump. He turned to face her, confusion and shock mingling with annoyance on his face.

"Sorry, it's just," She let go of his arm, her eyes wide as she stared up at him. "Do you know Allydia Cain?"

Phindi unlocked the door to open the gym for the day and did one final inspection of the equipment before taking her place behind the counter. She smoothed the front of her red tank top and sprayed the counter with disinfectant, wiping it down with a cloth. As she placed the cleaning supplies under the counter, a man with what looked like a newly-formed scab running across the bridge of his nose marched through the door. She stood upright, taking a defensive stance as she was all too familiar with men that carried themselves this way, chest puffed out, fists clenched, and jaw tight.

"You the owner?" the man in the baseball cap snarled.

She nodded, taking a pen from the cup on the glass counter, knowing it could be used to puncture his carotid, poke through his eye, or stab him in the hand should he grab her.

He lifted his shirt, revealing a small handgun tucked into the front of his faded jeans. "You should've minded your business, bitch." He reached for the gun as Phindi stepped back, keenly aware of her mortality, recent as it may be.

He pulled the gun and aimed it at her.

"What do have there, mate?" Navid asked as he strode in.

The man turned as the detective grabbed his wrist, squeezing so hard he dropped the weapon while Navid punched him in the solar plexus. He went down, the breath being forced out of him. Navid punched him in the nose, knocking him out cold.

"You all right, love?"

Phindi nodded, her mouth agape.

"Can I get one of them jump-ropes?" He gestured to the wall behind her where items for sale hung.

She tossed him a rope.

"Thanks." He rolled the man over onto his stomach and bound his hands, then his feet, hogtying the would-be assassin on the smooth gray floor. He called the local police and put his phone back in his pocket.

Phindi composed herself and smoothed her short hair. "I don't remember you being this attractive."

He raised his eyebrows. "Well, in my defense, the last time you saw me, I was starvin', dehydrated, and covered in my own blood. Have you seen my Gran? She's not answerin' calls or texts and her apartment's empty aside from the furniture."

"She moved in with Wyatt last month, though she's spent most of her time with him since becoming human. She's probably at their apartment. I will write the address down for you." She tore off a piece of blank receipt paper and scribbled the address on it before reaching across the counter to hand it to him.

He took it. "Thank you."

"Are you betrothed?"

"Betrothed?" he chuckled. "No, I'm not betrothed."

"Is there anyone you are courting for the purpose of eventual betrothal?"

"No, I'm not *courting* anyone at the moment."

"I am impressed with your skills in close combat and the efficiency with which you disarmed that man."

"Just job trainin'."

"The Queen mentioned. Detective, yes?"

"Yeah."

"You have a nice face and your body looks strong."

"Um, thanks?"

"Do you find me attractive?"

He raised his eyebrows again, feeling his shoulders tense. "Excuse me?"

"My face, is it to your liking?"

"Uh, yes, you're quite lovely."

"And, my body?"

"What?"

She stepped back and held her arms out to give him a better view. "Do you have a desire for it?"

He cleared his throat. "It would be ungentlemanly of me to comment."

"You are polite. That is a rare quality in a man. And, your accent is very charming."

"Phindi, is this your way of flirtin' with me?"

"Is it working?"

He pressed his tongue to the inside of his cheek. "Yeah."

"Would you like to have dinner with me?"

"I absolutely would."

"Excellent. I will seek your grandmother's permission and if she agrees, you will plan a date and text me the details. Is this acceptable?"

"Sure, but I'm fairly certain you don't need anyone's permission to date me but mine."

"I haven't dated a man without the Queen's consent since 1897."

"Oh."

"NYPD," an officer said as he and two others came through the door.

Navid showed him his badge and explained what happened while a female officer spoke to Phindi. She, too, explained the details of the incident.

"Navid was very brave and carried himself with dignity and strength." She looked past the officer and made eyes at her new suitor. He smiled back as the two male police officers laughed, mocking the suspect and nudging him awake. They dragged him out to the cruiser and threw him in the back while Phindi's interviewer placed the gun in an evidence bag.

"If you have any more problems, don't hesitate to call," she said as she left.

"Thank you," Phindi replied, but her eyes were fixed on Navid.

"I should go," he told her. "I really need to speak to my Gran."

"As do I."

"Right. I'll see you later."

"Yes, you will."

He left the gym, a smile plastered on his face. Phindi took her phone from under the counter and made the call.

Chapter 9

Allydia searched the bedroom for her phone. Her alarm hadn't woken her and Wyatt left her to sleep before heading to class which, even though she knew he meant it as a gesture of kindness, had aggravated her. What if something happened to him while he was gone? Or to her? She wouldn't have had a chance to say goodbye. It wasn't something that he thought about, but since becoming human again she was all too aware of how fleeting life could be. She wanted to make sure he always knew how much he meant to her...just in case.

The bedroom turned up nothing so she moved her efforts to the living room where she heard a faint buzzing come from the sofa. She slid her hand between the cushions and found the cell phone vibrating with an incoming call.

"Yes, Phindi," she answered.

"My Queen, I am calling to seek permission to pursue a romantic relationship with your relation, Navid. He has shown interest and has agreed to a social engagement of his choosing pending your approval."

"I see."

"Do you approve?"

She considered it, sitting on the couch and crossing her legs as she thought. "I have no objection. His private life is his own and you no longer answer to me. Date who you wish but I would caution you against bringing heartache to my grandson. I'm no longer your Queen but I am still fiercely protective of those I love, do you understand?"

"Of course your ma-- *Allydia*. Navid was here looking for you. It seemed urgent."

"All right, I'll call him now. Thank you." She ended the call and pulled up her grandson's number. "Phindi and Navid," she muttered to herself while the phone rang. "Eh, he could do worse."

"Gran?" he answered.

"Hello, Navid. Phindi said you were looking for me."

"Yeah, can you meet me at your old place?"

She stood, his tone causing her throat to go dry with anxiety. "Of course. Is everything all right?"

"I'm not sure. Just hurry, yeah?"

"On my way." She ended the call and rushed out the door, locking it behind her. *Meeting Navid at the old apartment,* she texted Wyatt, knowing he wouldn't see it until after school. *See you soon. Love you.*

Standing on the steps in front of Times Tower, Sinclair began to hyperventilate. Dozens of people passed by, some bumping into her as they walked. They were everywhere, milling about all with seemingly important places to be. Even the small children holding tightly to their parent's hands looked busy and the lights flashing all around were giving her a headache. It was loud, overcrowded, and chaotic. It was not a place she wanted to be.

She gripped the railing as she made her way down the steps, her mother's shoes, being a size too big, almost causing her to trip. She blew out a relieved breath when she got to the ground but the calm was swiftly replaced by an overwhelming sense of dread. Being part Nephilim, the sun didn't affect her the way it did a full vampire, but it still made her a little weak, her powers, as well as their side-effects, becoming stronger the older she got. As the dizziness grew, so did her inability to control her emotions. The heat from the late-morning sun felt hot on her skin. She tried to cover her neck with her hair, but it did no good, the radiation penetrating through her thick curls with ease.

She clutched her chest, her heart beating out of control and her stomach in knots. Hot tears spilled down her cheeks as she felt her knees starting to buckle. Her head felt like it would explode and the world around her went dim. She felt the hair on the back of her neck stand up as her hands began to tingle. She tried to stop it but she couldn't. The air around her snapped with the sound of electricity as her whole body sparked. As she battled herself, she heard her aunt's voice calling to her from a few feet away.

"Sinclair!" Gabriel raced to her, her presence instantly calming the trembling girl. The electricity dissipated as the angel took her niece's face in her hands. "Hey, you're okay. Look at me."

Sinclair locked eyes with her as her pupils fluctuated, growing to double their original size, contracting to normal and back to oversized in a matter of seconds.

"Okay, okay," Gabriel pulled her to her chest and wrapped her arms tightly around her. She kissed the top of her head and smoothed the back of her hair. "I'm right here. You're all right. You're all right."

Sinclair breathed in her aunt's scent, the chamomile and chocolate soothing her nerves as her heart rate slowly returned to normal.

Gabriel fought tears of her own as she continued to hold the girl. *Yo.*

Hello, sister, Lucifer replied. *You sound concerned. Is everything all right?*

A tear fell to her cheek. *Finish up your sightseeing. It's time to come home.*

Chapter 10

Blair fussed with the stippling brush, her full-coverage foundation doing little to cover the wrinkles around her eyes and mouth. No amount of makeup could hide how tired her eyes looked or how sunken her cheeks were. She did her best to make herself presentable, but she was embarrassed to show her real face, even to her own siblings. Yes, it was vain, and in the grand scheme of things, it mattered very little. Still, she obsessed, painting her face with more blush than was necessary in a sad attempt at looking younger. "I may be powerless," she muttered to herself. "But, I will *not* be ugly."

In the months since her coven's magic had been bound, all the spells they'd worked in the past had been undone. Her glamour was removed. Her brother was in the hospital, dying of a cancer she'd previously transferred to someone else. Unable to compel the townspeople to steal for them, the coven was running out of money fast. When the bank began threatening to foreclose on their house, three members left, getting jobs and sharing an apartment on Chestnut Street downtown. She'd felt betrayed but with her magic gone, she had no means of revenge. The remaining members mostly stayed in their rooms, finding it hard to look her in the eye, their impatience palpable.

Attempts had been made to undo the Tituban's binding spell, but no coven would dare help them and without magic, the Gowdies were as weak and pathetic as any other human. Blair wasn't just angry and mournful of the loss of her abilities, she was disgusted by what she'd become...normal.

As she finished applying a layer of lipgloss to her thinning lips, a knock came on the front door. She went downstairs to answer it, but before she'd made it to ground level, the door flew open as if by its own power and a man sauntered through, glancing around, his features twisted in disapproval.

"Who the hell are you?" she barked, preparing to turn and race back up the steps.

The pale man ran a finger along the banister before rubbing the dust from his skin. "You've really let the place go, haven't you?"

"The maid quit months ago. Who are you?"

He adjusted his jacket and looked her in the eye. "I'm a friend of Julia's. She came to you for assistance once. Do you remember?"

She scoffed, stepping down to stand directly in front of him, deciding that showing signs of fear was more dangerous than confronting a potential threat head-on. "The rejected Tituban? Yes, I remember." She felt lightheaded being this close to him. There was something odd about him, his presence alone causing her skin to crawl.

"Yes. You refused to help her. Now, she's dead. Had you provided her with what she asked for, she would have had the strength to withstand what I did to her. Sadly, with her magic stripped, she was left unprotected."

"What *you* did to her?"

"A necessary evil, as they say."

She took a step back. "What are you?"

A sickening smirk crossed his lips. "Old."

"What do you want?"

"I want you to give me what you deprived dear Julia of: assistance. It's the least you can do, given the fate she endured because of your selfishness."

She laughed. "There was no helping her. She was weak. I would have had to do her job *for* her. She was completely useless."

He snatched her up by the throat, lifting her from the ground with one hand as she struggled to breathe. His eyes flashed as his jaw tightened. "Julia was the vessel by which I entered this world. She freed me from captivity and by her blood, I was made flesh. Her sacrifice will not be forgotten and you will not insult her again."

Her feet dangled as the stench of sulfur filled her nose causing her eyes to water. The room grew dim as she choked, her painted nails clawing at his wrists. He dropped her, her knees hitting the floor as he crossed his arms.

"Clearly, you've lost your magic. The rest of your coven is as worthless as you are, I assume?"

She rubbed her neck and cleared her throat, casting him a defiant glare.

"Hmm." He stroked his chin as he thought. "Julia considered you to be the most powerful coven on this continent. She feared you."

"Everyone did," she coughed, getting to her feet. "But, as you said, we're worthless now. No magic, impoverished. My own brother's dying and I'm powerless to stop it. You want assistance? I have nothing to give."

He tilted his head, his features softening. "Would you like it back?"

"What?"

"All of it. The fear in a man's eyes when he realizes what he's up against. The control over others, including those in your coven. The magic. The *respect*."

She swallowed hard, his stare intense. "Of course, but--"

"I could restore you." He lifted her chin and turned her face to the mirror on the wall next to her. She gasped. Her wrinkles were gone. The bags under her eyes, gone. Her skin was bright and dewy, her lips full and smooth.

She put a hand to her cheek, unable to believe what she was seeing.

"I could give it all back, everything you've lost. I could make you whole. I could heal your brother and provide you with more money than you'd be able to spend in ten lifetimes. But, it would come at a cost."

She blinked a few times and turned again to face him. "A cost?"

He nodded.

"What is it that you'd want?"

He grinned. "Obedience."

Chapter 11

He could hear Annie screaming from the hall as he hyperventilated in the bathroom, pounding the back of his head against the door. He felt as though his mind was tearing itself apart, his reason floating away like a feather on the wind. He tried to pull himself together but his heart pounded so hard in his chest, he thought he might die. For a moment, he'd forgotten his name.

"Wyatt!" his wife called. "Wyatt, let me in!"

But, he wouldn't. He couldn't risk hurting her and no matter how many times she'd seen him like this, he still felt guilty for putting her through it. He knew she was afraid of him and the look on her face when he had these episodes broke his heart. Tears poured down his cheeks as he screamed, banging his fist on the side of his head.

Where are you? he heard in his mind.

He grimaced as if the sound hurt him. "Not now."

Tell me.

He screamed again, back fisting a hole in the closet door. "WYATT!"

He covered his ears in a feeble attempt to block out the noise.

Annie beat on the door, the concern in her voice now mingling with impatience. "I'm coming in!"

He got to his feet, stumbling to the sink where he splashed cold water on his face now flushed from the adrenaline coursing through his veins. As he patted his skin dry with the towel hanging on the ring above the light switch, he looked at the reflection staring back at him in the brushed nickel framed mirror. He jumped back, not recognizing the face of the man in the mirror. He had shoulder-length, blond hair, a square jaw covered by golden stubble, and eyes so blue they nearly glowed.

Wyatt squeezed his eyes shut. "It's not real." He took several breaths as he tried to settle himself. "It's another hallucination. *It's not real.*" But, when he opened his eyes, the strange face remained, peering at him from the other side of the glass.

Tell me where you are.

"Leave me alone!" he shouted. His chest heaved as he fought to catch his breath, the sound of his heart thumping so loud that he didn't hear his wife using a bobby pin to pick the lock. As she burst into the room, he yelled, "You're not real!", slamming his fist into the mirror, sending bloody shards crashing to the vanity below.

Wyatt was jolted awake by the automated announcement cutting through the white noise of the subway as it headed north. He rubbed the sleep from his eyes, pushing the memory from his mind and focusing his attention on the composition book in his lap, going over his notes from that morning's class. He hadn't thought about that day in years, the incident that finally chased Annie away. It felt like a lifetime ago but if he was being honest with himself, it was still too painful for him to think about. He had other priorities: Will, Allydia, and Sinclair. They, along with his siblings, were what mattered now. They were the ones that needed him. *No reason to dwell on the past*, he thought, his hands trembling as he turned the page and continued to read.

Gabriel had just dropped Sinclair off at home when she felt her brother's panic. She hurried back to the city, blowing through every stop sign and red light she came across. She flew into his apartment only a few seconds after he'd walked in, himself.

Relief washed over her as she took in his thoughts. "Oh, good. Just memories. I thought something bad happened."

"I'm fine." He closed the door behind her and took a seat at the island. "It's just been a while since I've had any dreams. You're jumpy, though."

She sat next to him. "Hazard of the job."

"Mm." He rested his elbow on the counter, his expression pensive. She rubbed his back while she waited for him to get out the words she knew he wanted to say. He gave himself a second before beginning. "You know, sometimes, for a second I'll think, 'What if this is all in my head? What if I'm really in a psych ward somewhere, drugged and strapped to a bed, hallucinating this whole life?' Because it's crazy, right? Demons and vampires, monsters, and angels. They're not supposed to exist. Maybe Annie didn't leave me, she just had me committed. But, then I look at Will or Allydia or you, and I don't care. What you've given me, *family* is everything. As twisted as it might be, I wouldn't trade it…even if it's imaginary."

Gabriel sniffed back the tears that threatened to come, the look in her brother's eyes crushing her like a tin can. She raised her hand and smacked him across the face, leaving a red mark on his cheek.

"Ow!" he laughed. "What was that for?"

"You felt that, right?"

He massaged his stinging face. "Kind of hard to miss."

"That's because *I'm real*. Dumbass."

Chapter 12

With their magic restored, the Gowdies skipped through town, emboldened, and out for blood. Blair gleaned as she watched her brother, now healed, blow up fire hydrants with the snap of his fingers. They cackled as water shot up and flooded the street, a rainbow forming in the air above.

They turned onto Chestnut, spotting the cars of their former members in front of the plain brick building, its black door leading to the apartment they now shared. A twisted grin spread over Blair's ruby lips as she held out her left hand, palm up.

"What are you thinking?" her brother asked as the others ran ahead into the building.

She smirked, raising her right hand and slapping it down onto her left causing the roofs of the cars to cave in, smashing the windows, their alarms ringing out into the otherwise quiet morning.

He laughed.

She brushed her hands together. "No escape now."

They joined the rest of the coven, racing up the steps to the third floor, the witches too impatient to wait for the elevator. In the hall, they waited for Blair to give the order. She led them to the apartment, raising a hand as if in greeting.

She turned to face them. "Show no mercy." She flicked her fingers, the door flying off its hinges into the living room where the three traitors sat drinking coffee.

"What the hell?" Kevin barked, nearly choking on his latte. Denise and Fiona just stared, the color draining from their faces as their hearts leaped to their throats.

The nine filed in, squawking and hissing as they blew out can lights and tore furniture apart with their bare hands.

"You betrayed my sister," Bennett explained. "Remind me, what's the punishment for abandoning one's coven?"

Kevin barreled toward him, balling his fists but Bennett threw him back with the flick of a wrist. He flew into the television, crashing into the screen and convulsing as electric current flowed through him. He fell face-first onto the floor, a puddle of foam escaping his lips as his eyes glossed over and the shaking stopped.

Fiona screamed, ducking behind Denise, the two now cowering in the corner. "Unsichtbar!" Denise yelped, but the women could still be seen.

Blair snorted. "Oh, *you* didn't get your powers back. Only loyal members of the coven were given back what was taken by the Tituban. *You* are traitors."

"Hey," Cyrus interrupted. "I don't mean to be a downer but is this necessary?"

"Excuse me?" Blair snapped.

"No disrespect but I mean, we're killing our own now?"

She glared at him, her nostrils flaring as she held herself back from slaughtering him, too. "They are *not* our own. *They abandoned us.* They left us when we needed them."

"Yeah, but--"

"But fucking nothing! They die. Those are the rules."

"The coven's rules or yours?"

"I *am* the coven! Now, get on board or you'll die, too." She faced the women again. "They'll get what they deserve."

Denise and Fiona screamed as the others pounced, clawing at their skin and gouging out their eyes. Blood and flesh fell to the ground in bits as the witches shrieked. Cyrus covered his mouth, horrified by what he was seeing. While everyone else was distracted, he slipped out and headed for the stairs. "Indespectus," he whispered, cloaking himself in an invisibility spell. He sprinted from the building, heading to the only place he thought might be safe.

"The Tituban," Cyrus said, clearing his throat as Poe opened the door. "Where is she?"

"Why would I tell you?" she asked, sensing his power. "And, how did you get your magic back?"

He looked behind him, feeling Blair's eyes on him even though she was nowhere to be seen. "Some guy Blair's taken up with. He's...off. Can I come in, please?"

She could tell that he was scared, which was odd for a Gowdie. She felt his magic, weaker than hers but only by a little. She was confident she could take him in a fight but it'd be close. "I guess." She let him in and locked the door behind him. "Why are you here?"

He coughed. "The coven's gone rabid. Blair's always been kind of fucked up but she's on another level, killing our friends." He cleared his throat again. "Everyone else is going along like it's normal. They're so happy to have their magic, they'll do anything she says."

"Didn't they always?"

He coughed into his elbow. "Yeah, but that was," He looked down at his sleeve, specks of blood now glistening on his skin. "They're coming." He flew through the house to the back door, rushing out into the garden.

"What are you doing?" she called, hurrying after him.

"I thought I saw some larkspur out here." His eyes darted around at the various plants and flowers. "There." He ran toward the blue and violet flowers but before he could reach them, he fell to his knees, hacking up blood and tissue as his lungs seemed to disintegrate.

"Subsisto cantamen!" Poe shouted over her guest's wheezing. He continued to cough, her spell having no effect.

He looked up at her with pleading eyes as she repeated the spell. Still, it did nothing. He grabbed her ankle. "Kill...her."

"Blair?"

He nodded. "And," he struggled to get out the words as he continued to choke. He pulled his phone from his pocket and showed her the screen. "That...guy." He bowled over, cups of blood followed by what looked like hundreds of dermestids pouring out of his mouth, the insects spreading over his face and devouring his flesh. Poe tried to bat them away but more came, leaving nothing left of his head but his skull.

She wretched, backing away as the bugs vanished before her eyes. "Goddamn Gowdies, man."

Chapter 13

Pearl chirped as she crawled over Wendy's open palm. The witch gently stroked the gecko's head and back, laughing to herself at how Gabriel would roll her eyes at the sight of the tiny creature playing on the kitchen island. "We eat here," she'd say. She didn't understand the witch/familiar bond and that was okay. Wendy didn't understand most of Gabriel's angel stuff, so they were even. She did feel like she was hiding something from her, though. Something was bothering her that she obviously didn't want to talk about. Wendy would let it go, for now. No sense starting an argument over something that was probably none of her business, anyway.

She jumped up, feeling the magic emanating from the hallway. She opened the door to see Poe, fist raised.

"Not even gonna let me knock?" Poe quipped.

"Sorry." Wendy closed the door and waited a few seconds before Poe tapped on the wood. She opened it again, a sly grin on her face.

"You're ridiculous."

"You're whiny," she giggled, letting the girl in and closing the door behind her.

"You finally got a familiar?" She sat at the island, touching a finger to the gecko's tail.

"Yeah, some dude was selling her on the street and she was so freakin' precious, I couldn't resist. What's up?"

"One of the Gowdies showed up at my house today."

She arched an eyebrow, sitting across from her. "Why?"

"They have their magic back."

"How? I bound them."

"Some guy." She slid the phone she'd taken off Cyrus' body across the counter, showing her the picture of the man. "He said there was something off about him. He asked me to kill him *and* Blair."

"His priestess? That's--"

"Treason, yeah. Something's going on, I'm telling you. He was scared and you know Gowdies. They're not afraid of anything."

"Where's your informant now?"

"Dead. Spelled. I tried, but I couldn't stop it. Whoever this guy is that's giving them power, he's *strong*."

Wendy examined the photo. "I don't recognize him. He does put off mad creeper vibes, though." She went to a drawer and got some ribbon and a pair of scissors. She wrapped the phone and did the incantation. When she was finished, she pursed her lips. "Hmm."

"What?"

"It didn't work. Here, help me out." She took Poe's hands and wrapped them around the phone, placing her own over them. She did the spell again and again and was still disappointed. "It's not working."

"How is that possible?"

She put her hands on her hips and bit her lip. "He's too powerful."

"How, though?" Poe wondered. "Not to be arrogant or anything, but aren't we like, the strongest witches ever?"

"Maybe not," she shrugged.

"We are, though. *You* are, at least."

She folded her arms and chewed on her lip as she thought. "Send the pic to the other covens. See if anyone's seen him before."

"Okay, but Wendy,"

"Hmm?"

"What the hell is this guy?"

Moloch winced at the sting of Wendy's spell. "Tituba," he seethed.

"What?" Blair asked.

He pushed her head back down. "I didn't tell you to stop."

She went back to servicing him while he rested his elbow on the arm of the solid gold throne he'd installed in the

Gowdies' formal living room, its snake embellishments winding around the legs and back. He watched the members of the coven indulging in the pleasures of the flesh on the floor, sofa, chairs, and chaise, mind-controlled townspeople doing as they were commanded. As amusing as the sexual escapades of humans were to watch, he grew perturbed. The Tituban that had bested Julia was now coming for him. This new threat along with the one he'd sensed upon his arrival in the States had him concerned. He needed more power.

He glanced over to the gold statues flanking the fireplace, their nude bodies and faces twisted in terror more arousing to him than the orgy he was witnessing or the woman's mouth around his genitals.

"What did you call them, again?" he asked.

Blair popped her head up, looking in the direction he was gesturing toward. "Oh, Denise and Fiona." She went back to her work as he smiled.

"That's right. Denise and Fiona. Just lovely." He closed his eyes and enjoyed the moment knowing that soon, he'd leave this place to acquire new allies, these more vengeful and depraved than even himself.

Chapter 14

Allydia stepped into her old apartment, barely getting the door closed before Navid rushed to meet her.

"What's wrong? Are you hurt?" she fretted, looking him over for signs of injury.

"No, I'm fine. Someone says she's got an important message for you and would only tell you in person. Made me bust her out of hospital."

"Hospital?"

He ushered her into the living room where Tamsen waited. She stepped forward, locking eyes with the former vampire. Allydia grunted, lunging at the girl who jumped back, falling onto the couch.

Navid stepped between them. "What are you doin'?!"

"She thinks I'm her," Tamsen said, standing and gesturing for him to step aside, her eyes still fixed on Allydia's. "Lilith's gone. I'm just Tamsen."

She wasn't convinced. "If she's gone, how are you standing?"

"Someone woke me up from my coma. It doesn't matter. I have to warn you."

She tilted her head. "Warn me?"

She nodded. "When Lilith was hurt and she thought the angels might find her here, she did a divination using the intestines from that guy."

"Tobin," she remembered, sorrow coloring her face as she crossed her arms.

"Yeah. She did the spell and found out that--"

"How do you know this?"

She shifted her weight from one foot to another, rubbing her arm as if she were cold. "I remember...everything. Everything Lilith knew, I know. Her plans, her spells, her," she grimaced as she swallowed. "Eating habits. Hell."

"And, you're still functioning? I'm impressed."

"The man at the hospital, I think he did something to me. I don't feel much of anything besides...calm."

"You owe him a favor, then. The last person I saw Lilith vacate was such a mess, she gouged her own eyes out in the hopes of ridding herself of the images left in her mind."

"That's...horrifying. Anyway, she wanted to see if her plan to destroy the Gate would work, but instead, she saw something else."

"Something else?"

"Something that scared her so bad, she almost went back to Hell willingly."

Allydia rolled her eyes. "The only thing that ever scared Lilith was her brother."

"Her brother?" Navid asked.

"Lucifer."

"Oh, well, sure."

"Navid, can you please give us a minute?"

Allydia cast her an annoyed glare. "You can speak freely."

"It's all right," he said, kissing his grandmother on the cheek. "I've got a date to prepare for, anyway. See that she gets back to hospital when you're done talkin', yeah? I don't want to get thrown in American prison for kidnappin'." He left the room and the apartment, locking the door behind him.

"So," Allydia said. "What had my stepmother so anxious that you felt it necessary to bring to my attention? Crows feet? A man growing tired of her?"

Tamsen squinted. "This is why she called you 'flippant'."

She sighed. "Did she fear the wrath of my father? If so, you have nothing to worry about. He's no longer a threat to *anyone*."

She shook her head. "You should sit down."

Lucifer took one last peaceful stroll around the island, breathing in the fresh ocean air and feeling the sun on his face. He'd miss it here, the quiet and the nature. But, his sister had sounded worried when she'd all but ordered him back. Whatever was bothering her must have been something she couldn't, or just didn't want to, handle on her own.

He went into the jungle, far enough away from any of the locals that no one would see him take off. He glanced around to make sure he was alone and bolted up, hovering over the trees and reveling in the island's beauty for a final time. He flew off, away from this paradise and on his way home.

When Gabriel left, Wyatt made himself some lunch. As he ate his sandwich, he realized he'd never turned his phone back on after class. He took it from his jeans pocket and took a sip of soda while it powered on. He munched on chips while he went through his texts, one from Allydia saying she was meeting Navid and another from Valerie.

Malik and Will are in a meeting with a contractor and not answering their phones. Sinclair ran away again and I can't find her. Can you--

He stopped reading and bolted from his seat at the island to the front door. He was in such a hurry, he almost forgot to lock up. He knew something was going on with his granddaughter, but running away? He had to find her before she got hurt or worse, hurt someone else.

Chapter 15

"Why the hell are we in *Yonkers*?" Blair complained, the rest of her coven silent, they too wondering why they'd been dragged to this decrepit building, the long-abandoned power station giving them all chills.

"I need more allies," Moloch explained. "Ones with no regard for their physical well-being, willing to use brute force to carry out my wishes, no matter the cost."

"And, you'll find them here?" she scoffed. "In a graffiti-covered relic?"

"Not *in* it," he sneered. "Under it."

She scrunched her eyebrows. "Raising the dead is a risky game. I don't recommend it."

He snickered. "Not the dead. The *damned*. Now, be good little witches and fetch me some humans. Keep them docile until I return."

"How many?"

"As many as you can. Thousands. More."

A breath stuck in her throat. "I don't have the power to control that many people at the same time."

His eyes flashed as he grabbed her by the throat. Her skin became ashen as her eyes went black. He pulled her close and through gritted teeth, he whispered, "Yes, you do." He let her go, smiling as she walked off to do his bidding. The others were hesitant, but with a flick of her wrist, they followed.

Once alone, Moloch entered the building, the shuffling of his brown and gray jackboots on the damp floor echoing through the room. After a few moments of searching, he finally felt it. "There you are." He closed his eyes and focused his power through his hands. At first, the gate to Hell was only made visible, the closed portal looking like little more than a void in the fabric of space. But, as he concentrated, sweat dripping from his pores, it slowly started to unravel, shattering like glass under the weight of his command. With one final push, the gate to Hell blew apart, revealing a crater of unknowable depth. He laughed as he caught his breath, relaxing his arms. He took a few seconds to prepare himself, restoring his energy and mustering his courage. Even for him, this wouldn't be easy.

"I hope this is all right," Navid said, pulling out a chair for Phindi. She sat, looking up at him in approval.

"It's very nice," she told him. "I especially like the charming portrait of the dog." She pointed up to the black-and-white painting hanging on the wall next to the table. He chuckled as he sat across from her.

"I haven't spent much time in New York, so I didn't know where a good place to eat was. I just did an internet search of romantic lunch spots in Brooklyn and this was the first place that popped up." He glanced around at the white-painted brick, wooden columns, and exposed pipes. "It's a lot more industrial than I thought it'd be."

"It's what they call 'trendy'. I don't know that I'd consider it romantic, but I do like the atmosphere. I have very high hopes for this place and for this date."

He shifted in his seat. "No pressure, right?"

"There is no reason to be nervous," she said. "My attraction to you grows by the minute."

He cleared his throat. "Thank you."

"Do you like my dress?"

"Yes, it's very nice."

"It is lilac, a bright color to catch your attention."

"I see," he said, taking a sip of water.

"And, it is low-cut to draw your eye to my exposed cleavage."

He choked, almost having to spit his water back into the glass.

She looked over the menu. "Do you know what you want?"

He skimmed the menu and nodded. "Yeah."

She rested her chin on her fist and flashed a sly smile. "So do I."

His eyes widened as he chugged the rest of his water.

"What can I get you?" a waiter asked, too overwhelmed by the lunch rush to notice the sparks flying at the table.

"I'll have a Caesar salad with grilled chicken," Phindi answered, her gaze still fixed on her date.

"The same," Navid said. "And, can we get an order of truffle parm fries?"

"Sure thing," the waiter said, hurrying off.

Their food arrived within minutes, each taking fries from the shared plate in between bites of salad and sips of soda. They talked about work and current events, laughing at each other's jokes and enjoying one another's company.

"So, you exploded the van?" she asked, clearly impressed.

He shrugged.

They both laughed. When it was time for dessert, they exchanged longing glances over molten chocolate cake, spooning bites into their mouths as they stared at each other.

"There is only one test left," Phindi said, breaking the silence between them.

"Test?"

"Of compatibility."

"Ah."

"So, you agree?"

"Agree to what?"

"We must engage in sexual congress."

He dropped his spoon and looked around the busy restaurant to see if anyone had heard.

"Am I making you uncomfortable?"

"No, no," He cleared his throat again. "I just--"

"We should do it now while I am fully aroused and freshly shaven."

He swallowed hard before waving to the waiter. "Check, please!"

They burst through the door of Phindi's loft, kissing passionately and tearing at each other's clothes. By the time the door was shut, they were naked aside from their undergarments, which quickly fell away as well. They collapsed onto the murphy bed, not bothering to get under the covers. He rested himself between her legs as they made out, his lips moving from hers to her neck. She ran her fingers through his soft hair, anticipating the moment of his entry when her body suddenly stiffened. She yanked his head back to look him in the eye.

"Do you have a condom?"

His face fell. "Oh, bollocks. I don't, I'm sorry. I didn't want to presume." He pushed himself off of her and sat up.

"It's all right, I have some in the medicine cabinet." She got up and went to the bathroom to fetch them. She tossed him the box. "I was warned that disease is rampant now, so I bought those, just in case."

"That's smart thinkin'," he said, ripping open the package and putting on the condom. "I'm clean, but--"

"I haven't been with a man since becoming human," she blurted.

"Uh, all right."

"I tell you this because I am not sure of my strength."

"Your--"

"I fear I may hurt you in my exuberance."

"Oh," he pulled her back down onto the bed and covered her body with his. "I wouldn't worry about that, love. I'm nothin' if not durable."

Chapter 16

The stench of sulfur filled obsidian halls as Moloch investigated the pit humans called Hell. Iron cages lined the walls, the coal floor leaving his boots filthy. A chill ran through him as he buttoned his suit jacket, surprised that he could see his breath. "The rumors aren't true, then," he said to no one in particular as he peered through the bars of various cells. "It's not hot at all down here."

"Who are you?" A voice came from behind.

He turned to face what he assumed to be a demon, his shape that of a man with a mutilated face and leathered skin the color of a rotting apple. His nose appeared flat against his face as though it had been crushed and his eyes shined like a cat's in an unnatural shade of gold.

"Are you in charge here?" Moloch asked.

"For now. How did you get in here?"

"Destructive ingenuity. I'm Moloch."

"Belphegor. Aren't you one of the false gods of the Canaanites?"

"*False?*" He adjusted his jacket and cracked his neck. "That's insulting. Just because your father *technically--*"

Belphegor's patience ran thin. "*Why are you here?*"

He sighed. "I've come to make you an offer." He held his arms out toward the cages. "All of you."

Voices from inside the cells began to chatter.

"An offer? From a defunct pagan deity?" He scoffed, the demons surrounding them cackling as they banged on their cell doors. "You have nothing."

"On the contrary," Moloch snapped his fingers, popping open every cage in Perdition. Demons flooded the halls, their ill-formed bodies packed in the space like taupe and onyx raisins. "I have everything I need...almost."

"Get back in your cells!" Belphegor boomed, but the demons resisted.

"We want to hear what he's got to say!" one of them shouted. Cheers erupted from the crowd in varying levels of shrill.

Moloch flashed a sleazy grin as he addressed the horde. "How long has it been since you've breathed clean air? Seen the light of the Sun? Felt the touch of a woman?"

The crowd grumbled.

"Would you like to once again?"

His question was met with raucous agreement.

"I can give you the world! Your jailer thinks I have nothing to offer but I can free you, break your shackles and lead you to a future where we make the rules. We decide who is and isn't worthy of the thing so brutally taken from you: *life*. *Life* is what I have to offer."

"How?" a demon called from the masses.

"By joining me. You will be my army as I rule over the Earth as its King. Elohim cast you out but stand with me and the world will be yours!"

The crowd again cheered, thousands of voices merging as one deafening screech.

"Wait, wait, wait!" Belphegor said. "How did you open the gate? Once it's been locked, only God can unseal it."

"God or *a* god. And, I didn't *unseal* it. I dismantled it entirely. The gate has been obliterated."

His gleaming eyes widened. "Everyone back in your cages! *Now!*"

Moloch rolled his eyes, making a fist as Belphegor's head caved in on itself. Soon, his whole body was pulverized, reduced to a compressed heap on the soot-covered floor. For a few seconds, all of Hell was silent. Then, more cheers along with applause rose from the mob. They celebrated, freedom finally within reach.

Still in her cage, Lilith trembled, holding it shut even as others tried to let her out. Her bright eyes shown through the tar-like substance that coated her as she watched the demons rally. She squeezed them shut, memories of what she'd seen when last she was on Earth playing in her mind like a movie reel. She shivered, gripping the bars as the others made their way to the newly-destroyed gate. As Hell grew quiet, she crumpled to the floor, balling herself up and hugging her legs. If the body she'd conjured for herself were real and functioned as such, she would have cried.

Phindi and Navid lay panting next to each other on sweat-soaked sheets, the blanket bunched up at their feet. Pillows, once at the head of the bed had been tossed to the floor, discarded as a hindrance to movement. They stared blankly up at the ceiling, limp, both too spent to care about the buzzing of a phone coming from the pile of clothes a few feet away.

"My legs are numb," Phindi said between heavy breaths. "That was amazing."

Navid nodded in agreement, still unable to form words.

"Did you enjoy it?"

He blinked a few times and let out a slow breath. "Immensely."

"That is a relief."

"A relief?"

"Yes, because I will want to do it again very soon."

"You and me both, I'd say."

"Excellent. I just need a twenty-minute nap first. I haven't been this fatigued in the day since I was a vampire."

He angled his head to look at her. "Do you miss it, bein' a vampire?"

She returned his gaze, rolling onto her side to face him. "I used to. When my queen stripped me of my power, my immortality, I was angry. I felt betrayed. But, I quickly came to appreciate the gift she'd given me...*freedom*. Freedom to be whomever I choose, to do as I see fit. I had been fighting one battle or another since my father trained me as a warrior. I was born for war. I was bred for it. I had never known another way. Now, I do as I please." She traced his bicep with her finger. "The first time your grandmother saved me, pulled my dying body from the battlefield, she gave me a new life in service to her. The second time, by restoring my humanity, setting me free, she saved my soul."

He rolled over and brushed her cheek, his fondness for her evident to her by the look in his eyes. "I'm glad you're happy."

She touched his hand and held it to her face while she spoke. "We are compatible, yes?"

"I think we are."

She smiled sweetly before kissing him, climbing on top of him, and reaching for the last condom on the nightstand.

"I thought you needed a nap?"

"Sleep can wait," she said, tearing open the wrapper and sliding the condom over him. "You should not have to."

Chapter 17

"Okay, Pearl, time for a snack." Wendy put the gecko in her terrarium before taking six mealworms from the plastic container and dropping them in the food dish. The lizard chirped and scurried toward the dish to feed. From the other side of the apartment, Wendy heard the front door open and close.

"Babe, are you home?" Gabriel called, setting her keys and phone on the kitchen island.

"Yeah," she called back, going to meet her.

Gabriel looked relieved as she grabbed her girlfriend's face and kissed her hard, pulling away abruptly and sitting on a stool. "I have to talk to you."

"You okay?" She sat next to her, covering her hand with hers.

"Not really." She squeezed her hand before patting the back of it and letting it go. There's something I haven't told you."

"I figured. You've been acting a little sus lately."

"I'm sorry."

"Angel stuff?"

She nodded. "I wanted to tell you. I *needed* to talk about it but," She put her fingers to her temple, closing her eyes and gritting her teeth at the sudden searing pain. "Fuck me."

"Headache? Do you need some--"

She grunted, shaking her head. "There's nothing you can do." Her eyes flew open and fixed on the door. "Oh, shit."

"What?"

The door flew open, Allydia storming in, a look of terror covering her ashen face. Tamsen came in behind her, hovering in the foyer.

"What's wrong?" Wendy asked the former vampire. "You look like you've seen ten ghosts."

"Tamsen," Gabriel said. "This is Wendy. She's a witch."

Wendy did a double-take. "We're just announcing that shit to strangers now?"

She ignored her question, doling out instructions. "Give her all of Lilith's spells. She's gonna need them. Wendy, when she's done put her in a cab to her parents' place upstate. Dia, get Michelle and Navid. Take them to the Southport house. The city's not safe." She stumbled to a kitchen drawer and took out a notebook and pen, handing them to the silent girl. Tamsen sat at the island and began to write.

"Will Wyatt survive this?" Allydia croaked.

She looked her in the eye, her expression hard. "I don't know, yet."

Allydia bit her lip, a single tear dropping from her eye as she hurried out of the apartment, slamming the door and racing to the elevator.

"Okay, what the fudge?" Wendy asked.

"It's too late," Gabriel said, wincing in pain as she grabbed the sides of her head. "I can't explain." She fell to the floor, squeezing her eyes shut as blood dribbled from her nose. She clutched her stomach as she curled herself into a ball, taking shallow, labored breaths.

Tamsen took a quick glance at the angel on the floor, barely registering the scene as she continued to write.

"Gabriel!" Wendy knelt next to her. "Percuro!" she demanded. "PERCURO!"

The spell was useless. Gabriel continued to writhe in unimaginable pain, going pale and coughing up blood.

"It's okay," Wendy cried, retrieving the phone from the counter. "I know what to do."

Lucifer coasted at a leisurely pace over the Atlantic, enjoying the view of the ocean beneath him. In the distance, he could just make out the iconic New York City skyline, the Empire State Building like a beacon calling him home.

He felt his phone buzz in his pocket and took it out, seeing it was Gabriel that was calling. "Sister," he answered.

"Don't be impatient. I can almost see your apartment from here."

"Lucifer, it's Wendy," the voice on the other end quivered.

He stopped where he was, floating over the water at an altitude too high for ships to see him. "What's wrong, love? You sound distraught."

"Something's wrong with Gabriel. She had a headache and then she grabbed her stomach and she's coughing up blood and, oh, God!"

"What? What is it?!"

"I think she's having a seizure!"

He looked toward the city and shoved his phone back in his pocket, taking off so fast, he created a sonic boom.

Chapter 18

Tamsen had retreated to the guestroom to finish her work by the time Lucifer arrived, flinging open the balcony door and rushing to crouch next to Gabriel on the floor.

"How long has she been like this?" he asked, placing a hand on her forehead.

"Ten minutes, maybe," Wendy told him, her voice shaking as tears streamed down her face.

"She's burning up."

"What's wrong with her?"

He pursed his lips.

"Why aren't you doing anything? Help her!"

"I can't."

"Why the hell not?! You fixed me when I was hurt. Doesn't your angel healing shit work on illnesses?"

"This isn't a sickness, pet. She's receiving the wo--"

Gabriel stopped moving, stopped breathing, her body limp on the hardwood.

"Hey," Wendy whimpered, lightly slapping her girlfriend's cheek. "Wake up."

"It's all right, love," Lucifer assured, his voice barely above a whisper.

"Get up," she sobbed. "Get--"

Gabriel's eyes flew open as she sucked in a deep breath. Lucifer sighed in relief, standing as Wendy threw her arms around her neck. "I thought you were dead."

"Just for a second," she said, pulling away, her eyes wide as she stared up at her brother. "Lucifer," She stood, taking his hand and placing it on her head. "Listen."

He closed his eyes as he took in her thoughts, his pulse quickening and his hands going clammy. His mouth fell open as he stumbled back, catching himself on the island.

She wiped the blood from her mouth and went to the fridge, getting a bottle of water. She took a long swig and replaced the cap while the others stared after her.

"Are you okay?" Wendy asked, still shaking with nerves.

"Ish." She walked back to kiss her on the cheek before turning her attention to her brother who was barely holding himself upright. She tilted her head, giving him a knowing look. "I need a ride."

"Did you find her?" Wyatt asked as Valerie met him at the front door, letting him in and closing it behind him.

"Yeah," she told him. "Gabriel brought her home hours ago but she went right to her room and won't come out. I'm worried about her. I thought it was just normal teenager bullshit but for a second today, she had fangs. That's never happened before. And, she's drawing some really fucked up shit."

"I saw. What does Gabriel say?"

She rolled her eyes, leaning on the banister, and smacking her lips. "She just said, 'hang tight' and hee heed into the wind. I swear, that bitch has been on my every last for months, acting like she knows better than *me* how to raise *my* child."

"Yeah," He said, hugging his arms, remembering when she'd given Will a computer when he was five and the many lectures she'd given him about stifling his development. "She did the same thing with Will. The thing was, though, as much as it aggravates me to say,"

"She wasn't wrong." She sighed. "I know. She never is. That's what makes it so annoying."

Wyatt nodded. "You mind if I talk to her?"

She shrugged. "Give it a shot. She just yells at me to leave her alone. Maybe she'll respond better to you."

He'd taken the first step up the staircase when he felt a tremor. "Does Connecticut get earthquakes?"

"Not any we should be able to feel." She gripped the banister as the shaking went from barely detectable to strong enough that the chandelier rattled. "What the--"

From her room, they heard Sinclair scream. They started up the steps but were nearly knocked over as Gabriel rushed in and bolted past them.

"Get them out of here!" she called to Lucifer hurrying in behind. Without hesitation, he gripped the two by their arms and dragged them from the house at hyper-speed. Standing in the yard, he blocked them as they attempted to get back inside.

"Move!" Valerie shouted as he held her back.

"I can't," he said, holding her by the shoulders and staring into her eyes, the tone of his voice giving her pause. "I'm sorry."

The ground quaked again, setting off Wyatt's car alarm. He took his keys from his pocket and turned it off. "The hell's going on, Lucifer?"

"We need to stay here," he said, shifting his gaze to Wyatt while keeping a firm hand on his sister's shoulder. "Trust me, brother."

He pursed his lips, rubbing the stubble on his face and folding his arms. "I might be crazy, but I think I do."

Valerie again tried to push past him. "If you don't get out my way, I swear to fuck, I will Holy Fire your ass into motherfuckin' oblivion."

"You must trust me, Uriel," Lucifer said, the look of compassion in his eyes confusing her more. "I won't let anything happen to you."

Inside, Gabriel burst into the bedroom to find Sinclair convulsing on the floor, blood spewing from her mouth and nose. "Hey," she said, inching into the room. "Hey, I'm here. I'm right here."

"Gabriel," the girl choked as she fought to stop the trembling.

"Yeah." She knelt next to her, holding her hand and kissing her on the forehead. "I'm right here with you."

"I'm afraid," she said, her voice barely above a whisper as tears spilled down her cheeks.

"I know." Tears gathered in Gabriel's eyes, too as she did her best to appear strong. "It'll be over in a minute."

Sinclair's face twisted in pain and she screamed again, bolts of white-hot lightning shooting out from her body in all directions. Gabriel was thrown back into the chalkboard wall, her head splitting the drawing of a neon billboard in two. She fell to the floor, holding a hand up in front of her to deflect the barrage of electrical discharges being flung from Sinclair's changing body.

The sound of snapping bones cut through the girl's cries with an eerie resonance while skin and muscles stretched. Fangs grew and receded as her eyes flashed black. Lightning struck the bed and curtains, starting fires that grew too fast for Gabriel to put out while she deflected bolt after bolt, her telekinesis the only thing preventing her from being struck again.

What's going on? Wyatt sounded in her head. *I see smoke.*
It's all right, she replied. *We'll be out in a second.*

A flood of electricity poured from Sinclair's solar plexus, Gabriel barely able to keep it from engulfing her in a plume of pure energy. She closed her eyes as the intense light crept up and around her. The house shook, pictures and light fixtures falling from their places, smashing on the hardwood below.

Opening her eyes just enough that she could see, Gabriel took one last look around the room she grew up in, taking a mental photo as she said to herself, "Can't say I'll miss it." Bits of plaster broke free from the ceiling as Sinclair's howls intensified. As the lightning subsided and the girl went quiet, a beam came crashing down, filling the air with a cloud of drywall dust.

Outside, the three siblings waited, the brothers watching the house from the grass as Valerie paced on the sidewalk behind them. Wyatt held his arms, biting his lip as Lucifer attempted to comfort him.

"Gabriel will be fine," he said, patting his shoulder.

"And my granddaughter? Will she be all right?"

He tipped his head and raised an eyebrow. "I suppose that depends."

"On what?"

"Your definition of 'all right'."

From the house, they heard what sounded like an explosion. Windows blew out as the roof caved in on itself, waves of lightning ripping through the air above them. Valerie covered her face and dropped to her knees while Wyatt took a step forward. "I'm going in."

Lucifer grasped his arm. "You mustn't."

"Let go."

"Do you remember what happened last time you were hit with a jolt like that?"

"I survived."

"Do I have to remind you that your vampire sweetheart is no longer a vampire? Should she die, a burning similar to the one you received from your son will send Barachiel straight back to Heaven and Wyatt will cease to be."

"The odds of that happening are--"

"It doesn't matter how slight the chances, I will not risk it. Come Hell or high water, you will live to see the end of this day."

Another boom shook the house, this one too strong for the foundation to withstand. The building crumbled before them, reduced to a pile of rubble as Lucifer moved to shield the others from the fallout.

"Sinclair!" Valerie yelped as her brother held her back.

Smoke and dust filled the air, the sudden silence the loudest thing Wyatt had ever heard. *Gabriel,* he called in his mind. No answer. *Gabriel!* His chest tightened, his eyes darting around, unable to see through to where the building used to stand. Finally, behind the cloud of ash came the sound of his sister coughing.

I'm fine, she answered. *Just clawing my way of out my damn childhood.*

As the dust settled, two figures appeared. In front, a grown Sinclair, her mother's clothes, oversized just a few minutes before, now fitting perfectly. Gabriel followed, brushing dust from her pants.

"Damn it," she complained. "These pants are ruined. You know how hard it is to find pants this comfortable?"

"Not really," Sinclair giggled.

"They are *yoga* pants that look like *dress* pants. *Boot-cut.* I'm gonna have to scour the internet--"

"Baby?" Valerie said, rushing to her daughter, holding her face in her hands as she looked her over. "Are you okay?"

She smiled and nodded.

Valerie let out a sigh of relief as she hugged her. "So, this is it?" She pulled away and gave her another once-over. "You're done growing?"

"Yeah, I'm done."

"How do you feel?" Wyatt asked, remembering how scared Will had been when he'd grown to adulthood overnight.

"Honestly?" She put her hands on her hips. "Hungry."

"Well, let's get you something to eat, then." Valerie turned to walk to her car but was stopped by a change in Wyatt's expression. He looked confused. "What?" She followed his glance and saw Lucifer, a tear sliding down his cheek as he stared, transfixed by the woman in front of him.

"I'm sorry," he said, his voice quiet, averting his eyes.

"Just breathe," Gabriel told him, her compassionate tone causing Valerie and Wyatt to exchange baffled looks.

Another tear fell from Lucifer's eye as he put a shaky hand to his chest, breathing out slowly as he dropped to his knees. He sniffed back more tears as he bowed his head. "Forgive my staring. I was overwhelmed. I didn't think I'd ever see you again...Father."

Valerie grabbed Wyatt's arm to steady herself, both taken aback at what they were hearing.

Sinclair lifted Lucifer's chin, looking him in the eye.

He trembled as more tears fell. "I've failed you."

"You've done no such thing." She took his hand and pulled him up, wiping the tears from his face. "You're exactly where you're meant to be."

Wyatt's legs went numb, his mouth going dry, and his heart racing. "Sinclair?"

She turned her head, smiled at him, and winked.

Chapter 19

Wyatt drove back to the city, Gabriel next to him and Sinclair in the backseat, dreamily looking out the window like she didn't have a care in the world. His knuckles were white around the steering wheel, his jaw clenched. He stared ahead, ignoring the awkwardness of the silence in the car.

Gabriel tapped her fingers on her knee, biting her tongue and rolling her head on the back of her seat. When she couldn't take her brother's frustration anymore, she let out an exasperated sigh. "I'm sorry I didn't tell you."

He kept his eyes on the road, his head tilting slightly as he decided to stop ignoring her. "Why didn't you?"

"I don't make the rules."

His steely glare moved to Sinclair's reflection in the rear-view mirror then back to the road. "How long have you known?"

"Are you kidding me?" Gabriel removed a chunk of debris from her hair. "I'm gonna be pulling this shit out of my hair for weeks."

"How long?"

She bit her bottom lip and cleared her throat. "Since Michelle brought her to me."

"A year?" He shook his head. "Her whole life."

"I'm sorry!"

"Would you have loved me the same if you'd known?" Sinclair chimed in.

He looked in the mirror at her again.

"Would you be in school, working toward a goal, starting a new career? Would you be happy and content as you are now, or would you have spent the last year worried about why I was here, crippled by dread and letting life pass you by like cars on the highway?"

Gabriel plucked more drywall from her chestnut locks. "She's got you there."

He cast her an annoyed side-eye.

"Besides," Sinclair clarified. "I'm not really *here*, here. I'm still asleep. My subconscious is just kind of borrowing Sinclair's body. It's like I'm in a lucid dream."

"I just saw Lucifer grovel at your feet like a dog," he dismissed. "You're definitely here."

She chuckled. "He's a good boy."

Gabriel snickered.

"Because you said 'dog' and Lucifer's my boy, like, my son. You get it."

He flashed his sister an unamused glance.

"Dad jokes, remember?"

He rolled his eyes. "I thought with the Gate closed, nothing but human souls could get in or out."

"'Nothing' doesn't really pertain to me. However, had it been destroyed, I wouldn't have been able to repair it until I woke up, which means I wouldn't be able to be here now."

"Why *are* you here?"

She went back to looking out the window. "When we get back. For now, I'd like to enjoy the ride."

Lucifer sat in Valerie's passenger seat as she followed the others to Gabriel's apartment. He'd started to calm down, though his hands still had a slight tremble.

"She's God?!" Valerie blurted, cutting the quiet like a chainsaw.

"Settle yourself, sister. Wouldn't want to cause an accident."

"God?!"

"Just a bit of Him."

"Which bit?"

He chuckled.

"And, if Sinclair's God, is she even Sinclair? Is she a real person at all? What the fu--"

"I'm sure He'll explain."

She glanced over at him, her features softening. "How are you?"

"Me?"

"Yeah. This must be another level of fucked up for *you*. Are you okay?"

He thought for a moment. "Do you know what? For the first time in a very long time, I think I am."

Chapter 20

"Navid!" Allydia pounded on the door of Phindi's loft. "Navid, I tracked your phone! Let me in!" When no answer came, she used the key she'd been given for emergencies and opened the door herself. She found the two scrambling to put their clothes back on and turned her back, an exasperated sigh escaping her lips.

"Boundaries, Gran!" Navid shouted as he zipped his trousers.

"I apologize but you weren't answering your phone."

"Kind of busy." He threw on his shirt while Phindi adjusted her dress.

"Is everything all right?" Phindi asked.

"No," she said, peeking over her shoulder to make sure they were decent before turning to face them. "Elohim has returned."

Navid's jaw dropped. "Isn't that--"

"Yes."

Phindi put her hand to her heart. "The Creator?"

"Yes. We have to go."

"Go?" Phindi asked. "Where could we go to hide from God?"

"We're not hiding from God, I don't think. His Messenger told me to get you somewhere safe, so that's what I'm doing. We just have to pick up Wyatt's daughter-in-law first. Get your shoes on."

Navid fumbled as he tied his laces. "Gabriel told you? Is she all right?"

"She's fine," Allydia said, casting him a suspicious glare.

He rolled his eyes.

"What are these looks?" Phindi asked, gesturing between them.

Allydia tapped her fingers on her arm.

"It's nothing," Navid insisted.

Phindi raised an eyebrow.

"Really. I had a *mild* crush. *Had*, past tense."

Allydia tossed her hair over her shoulder. "I never approved."

"You were involved with the angel?"

"No. It was just a crush."

Allydia scoffed.

"*Fine*, we made out, briefly, *once*. Pants were on the entire time."

The women were silent.

"I've had two girlfriends since then, not including you." He touched Phindi's arm. "I do not still have a thing for Gabriel. I swear."

"I warned Phindi not to hurt you," Allydia told him, turning to lead them out of the apartment. "But, if you treat her badly, I'll slap *you* around a little, as well."

After new-student orientation, Michelle wandered the campus grounds, admiring its buildings, some of which were over three hundred years old, and breathing in its rich history. She spent hours in the natural history museum, prying herself away only when she'd realized she'd skipped lunch and was starving. She leaned against the massive stone a sculpture of a triceratops stood on as she took one last look around, smiling to herself. "Tae would be proud," she said under her breath, the quiet breeze feeling like peace against her skin. "This is where I belong."

"Michelle!" she heard in the distance, breaking her contemplation.

She stepped away from the stone and onto the sidewalk indented with dinosaur-shaped paw prints and saw Allydia, her grandson who she hadn't seen since her wedding, and the ex-vampire Will had shocked months earlier. "Allydia? What are you doing here?"

"Ivy League," the former vampire approved. "Wise choice."

"Thank you. It's the closest school to Sinclair that I got into."

"I don't think that need be a consideration anymore."

"What?"

"We must go now. Come."

"Why? What's going on?"

"Just come. I don't know how much time we have and you're making a scene."

"Old woman, I will *show you* making a scene if you don't tell me what's happening *right now.*"

Allydia tilted her head and arched an eyebrow. "Rude," she scolded. "But, fine." She glanced around to make sure no one was in earshot. "Elohim has returned in the form of your daughter. I don't know the details as to why but Gabriel instructed me to fetch you and get you to safety and I learned long ago that her Father isn't one to be trifled with, so *let's go.*"

Her jaw dropped, the color draining from her face as she remained motionless on the pavement.

Allydia huffed. "Phindi, be a dear?"

She nodded, rushing forward and throwing the girl over her shoulder. They hurried back to the car, piling in and speeding away, on their way to the airport and to safety.

On the plane, Michelle made several frantic attempts to get in touch with Will. Every call was sent straight to voicemail, every text left unseen. "Fucking contractors," she muttered.

Allydia and Phindi chatted while Navid sat opposite them, mesmerized by his new girlfriend's graceful movements. She smoothed her baby hair and dragged her fingers down the side of her face, over her chest, and to her lap where she folded her hands, never taking her eyes off her former queen. She listened intently to every word spoken before responding, her words always honest, clear, and direct. There were no games with her. She meant every word she said and spoke with abandon, unafraid to ask for what she wanted or to be exactly who she was. She was spectacular. *Don't be an idiot*, he thought. *You've spent one day with the girl. It's way too early to be catching feelings.* But, as he watched her, he couldn't help but feel like this relationship would be different because *she* was different. Unlike the women he was used to dating, she was unabashed, genuine, and forthright. She was real. No matter how much he tried to dismiss his emotions as ridiculous, a strange knowledge had come over him, a sixth sense of sorts. He knew it in his bones. She was the one.

For a moment, their eyes met causing his heart to flutter. They exchanged smiles before she went back to her conversation and he looked down at his phone. He scrolled through his pictures, found the one Gabriel had taken of herself, and deleted it.

Chapter 21

Sinclair finished her fifth pudding cup and took a bite of her peanut butter and strawberry jam sandwich. "I've been craving one of these all day." She took the sandwich with her, eating as she rifled through Gabriel's pantry for more snacks. The others sat at the island, lined up on the side opposite the kitchen, watching in awkward silence. "Score," she said, grabbing a box of cinnamon cereal and shoving the last bit of sandwich in her mouth as she got a bowl from a cupboard.

"Would you like me to order you a proper meal?" Lucifer offered.

"Unnecessary." She dumped the cereal in the bowl, poured milk over it, got a spoon, and dug in.

Lucifer gave Gabriel a disapproving scowl. "This is your fault."

She shrugged. "Be grateful it's not blood."

"Don't bicker," Sinclair scolded.

"Yes, Father," Lucifer agreed.

"Sorry," Gabriel said.

Wyatt and Valerie exchanged surprised looks.

"So, are you gonna tell us what you're doing here or should we just guess?" Wyatt asked, evoking a stunned look from Lucifer.

She finished her cereal and placed her dishes in the sink before making her way back to the pantry. "Oh, you know, stopping a big bad, saving the world, same old, same old. Gabriel, do you have any," She grabbed a box of toaster pastries. "Never mind. Found them." She opened a pouch and put the pastries in the toaster.

Valerie took a deep breath as she gathered the nerve to ask, "So, are you still Sinclair, or are you strictly--"

"Hey, Dad," Will said, entering the apartment and closing the door. "I got your message to meet you here. That meeting took *forever*. What's u--" He stopped, seeing the woman in the kitchen that bore an uncanny resemblance to his daughter. "Sinclair?"

"Hey, Dad," she said as the pastries popped up. She took them out of the toaster and handed him one. "Hungry?"

He took it. "Starving." He took a bite. "Growth spurt, huh?"

"You could say that."

"Are you older than me?"

"Uh...yeah."

Gabriel giggled.

"Thirteen to thirty," Lucifer informed him. "He thinks He's funny."

"I'm hilarious," she defended. "I made a marine mammal that surfs in boats' wakes. They do it on porpoise."

Gabriel covered her mouth and laughed.

Will gobbled the last of his snack and got a bottle of water from the fridge. "Okay, I'm confused."

Wyatt stood, but before he had a chance to speak, Lucifer blurted, "She's God."

Wyatt smacked him upside the head.

Lucifer rubbed the back of his head. "What?!"

Sinclair flashed a stern look. "Barachiel, don't hurt your brother."

Will choked on his water. "She's what, now?"

"God," Sinclair told him, handing him a protein bar from the pantry.

There was a moment of silence while he processed. He took another sip of water and put the bottle down. "For how long?"

"Forever. Sinclair's human soul was in charge while she grew up, having her own experiences, living her life. I was in the background, mostly, poking my head out on a rare occasion."

He furrowed his brow. "Was she aware of you?"

"Of course. And, she's still in here, just," She pointed to her temple and clicked her tongue. "Taking a break. She's got to take a back seat while I get some work done. Speaking of work, Lucifer,"

"Yes, Father," he said, standing.

"I need the city evacuated. Now."

"As you wish." He hurried from the apartment, eager to please his Father.

"Uriel, take your sword to the roof and get comfortable with it again. You're a tad rusty."

She raised an eyebrow, not getting up from her seat. "It's kind of buried under a house right now."

Sinclair went to the fridge and pulled out a block of cheddar, tossing it to Valerie. "I guess you could fight with this."

She caught it, giving her a puzzled look.

Gabriel laughed.

Sinclair flashed an amused smile. "It's extra sharp."

Wyatt groaned as he slapped his palm to his forehead. Valerie sighed as she put the cheese back in the fridge and sat back down.

Sinclair picked a piece of lint off of Gabriel's shoulder and gave her an imploring look.

Gabriel sighed, waving her hand in the direction of the balcony doors, opening them with her mind. "I really wish you would've said something earlier." Sinclair smirked as Gabriel raised her hand. "People are gonna think they're seeing a damn UFO."

Through the open doors, the sword came whizzing in, spiraling through the air at breakneck speed. Will covered his head, ducking as Wyatt and Valerie leaned out of the way. Gabriel caught it by the hilt and held it out to Valerie who took it, shaking her head.

"I guess I better hop to, then," Valerie said, getting up from her seat. "Wouldn't want to piss off the Almighty."

Sinclair winked at her as she left and turned her attention back to Gabriel. "Take Wendy to Tarrytown. Have her gather the witches and teach them Lilith's spells. Oh, and Tituba's exorcising spell. Can't forget that."

Gabriel nodded in agreement. "Which witches?"

She finished her pastry, her eyes darkening as her tone became more serious. "All of them."

Gabriel stood and called over her shoulder, "You down?"

On the couch in the living room sat a petrified Wendy, clutching the notebook Tamsen had filled with Lilith's spells before going home to her parents. Her mouth hung open as she trembled, shakily getting to her feet and following her girlfriend out the door.

Sinclair waved goodbye and as the door closed, she met Will's stare. "I know you're upset but just in case I don't get a chance to tell you later, you've been a really good dad."

He scrunched his eyebrows, staring at her for a few seconds before dropping his water bottle in the trash can. "I need a walk."

"Will," Wyatt called after him, but Sinclair placed a hand on his shoulder, forcing him down onto a stool.

"He needs a minute."

Will slammed the door behind him, leaving his father alone with his daughter-turned-God. Wyatt glared at Sinclair who sat on the other side of the island, taking a sip of her water. He chewed the inside of his cheek as his mind raced, his shoulders tightening as he thought about what to say.

"We have some time," Sinclair said, replacing the bottle's cap. "Go ahead and ask."

He averted his glance. "It's probably not my place."

She laughed. "You're an archangel of the Lord. Your usual *place* is in the Throne Room of Heaven. You can ask me questions. You may not always like my answers but you are always free to ask."

He folded his hands in his lap and returned her gaze.

"You're wondering why I let bad things happen, why I don't just snap my fingers and fix the world's problems. You want to know why I let people suffer."

He let out a tentative breath, not wanting to offend God by daring to question Him but too curious to dismiss it. "Kind of."

She moved around the island to sit next to him, facing him as she spoke. "Have you liked every decision Will's made?"

"What?"

"When he wanted to marry Michelle so fast?"

"Well,"

"When he burned half a town to the ground? When he killed your father? When he killed *you*?"

His jaw tightened. "Did I *like--*"

"No, of course, you didn't. But, you loved him, anyway. You forgave him. And, if he did something equally as horrible at some point in the future, you'd forgive him again. You would love him through anything."

"Of course."

"And, when he was little and learning to ride a bike, did you hold onto his shoulders and keep him steady forever or did you let him fall?"

"I let go," he said, beginning to understand. "He had to fall a few times to learn to balance."

She brushed a stray hair away from his eyes. "He did. And, as he's your child, you are all mine. I love people as you love him. They're not pets to be trained. Human souls need freedom to learn and grow, just as you have."

"Me?"

She nodded. "You don't remember it but before you were Wyatt, you had become discontented. As Barachiel, you did as I asked but you were just going through the motions, saving people because I'd told you to and for no other reason. Your empathy had dwindled. For that reason and many others, I put you in Wyatt Sinclair, knowing what life would be like for you. I gave you the opportunity to not only see the best and worst of human existence but to *feel* it. To *know* it so that next time I command you to keep someone from jumping off a bridge, you'll sympathize with the pain they're going through. When I ask you to bless someone with a baby, you'll understand the joy it will bring to those parents, and when I tell you to save a child who would die if not for your protection, you'll do it wholeheartedly because you know the devastation of losing a child yourself."

His hands trembled as his heart beat out of his chest, his eyes wide with anger and shock. "You put me through hell for *job training*?"

"Yes, but I also put you in Allydia's path, so...you're welcome."

"*What?*"

"What Lilith did to her was atrocious, making her a killer, giving her the bloodlust. She never would have agreed to be saved like that if she'd been given the choice. Her kids got taken, her father abandoned her, and I had to let it happen. I needed her army to defend the Gate so I could slip through when Sinclair was born. I've always felt guilty about that so I had Gabriel introduce you."

"You had her...you orchestrated my relationship?"

"Don't get offended. I didn't manipulate your feelings. I just knew that if she met you, the part of her that was still *her* would fall hopelessly in love with you and that you would eventually love her, too. She would protect you and the others when you needed her to and your influence would give her the final push she needed to cure herself and unwittingly eliminate vampirism which would be one less thing for me to worry about and *then*, Allydia would have the life she always deserved. You would find joy and feel from her the unconditional love you hadn't known before as Wyatt. You would know what it meant to be someone's top priority and you would build a life with her that, over time, would eradicate the torment you sometimes still feel from your past. That love will heal you and sustain you for the rest of your time on this planet."

He blinked. "I don't know what to say."

She shrugged. "Say, 'Thanks, Dad'."

He laughed. "Thanks, I guess."

"Not the most sincere but I'll take it."

"I have another question."

"Sure."

"You basically just told me you planned for me to have Will but Gabriel said we can't--"

"Angels normally can't, which is another reason I needed you here. Only Barachiel could use the loophole."

"Loophole?"

"Annie prayed for a baby. As worried as she was about your presumed mental illness being passed on, she still wanted to be a mother more than anything. I knew that Wyatt would do anything to keep from losing her and Barachiel would be affected by that and he would answer her prayer. She got cold feet when she thought she'd have to choose between you and her son. Luckily for me, Nephilim grow fast."

"Wait, you're saying--"

"I'm only as strong as the body I'm in when I'm on Earth normally, let alone when I'm unconscious. It has to be that way. The last time I showed my true face, a guy climbed down a mountain thirty years older than when he'd climbed up. So, I needed to be half-Nephilim and half-vampire. It's the strongest combination of--"

"You puppet-mastered my son and his wife, too?!"

"*Again*, not their feelings, just their circumstances. I didn't make them fall in love, I just knew they would. I didn't make them have sex, I just made sure the pharmacist Michelle went to for the morning after pill would give her a box that expired almost ten years ago. I set that in motion before I went to bed."

His jaw dropped.

"What?" Outside, thunder clapped as the sky darkened. She looked to the window and smiled. "My baby."

Chapter 22

Thunder clapped so loud it rattled the windows of the cafe Will now sat in, sipping coffee and staring out the window onto the Hudson. He'd wandered from Gabriel's apartment down West 70th Street and stopped here when the rain started, hoping to wait out the storm that only seemed to grow in intensity.

His phone buzzed on the table, Michelle's image lighting up the screen. He picked it up, eager to speak to her. "Hey, I need to talk to you about something."

"Allydia told me," she said. "Sinclair's God?!"

"For now. Apparently, He came with her when she was born and she's known the whole time. I don't," He pinched the bridge of his nose and squeezed his eyes shut. "I don't understand why she never said anything."

"Maybe He wouldn't let her? Divine plan or some bullshit?"

"I don't know. He said she's still in there, still alive, still aware. I just hope when He's done doing whatever He needs to do, He gets the hell out of her and takes His all-knowing ass back to Heaven. I can't--" He stopped, noticing a couple listening in on his conversation with puzzled looks on their faces. "Anyway, how are you? Are you okay?"

"Not really but how could I be, right? Gabriel had Allydia drag me off campus and now I'm on a plane to Indiana while my family's in who knows what kind of danger. I'm with the chick that locked me in a cage, another ex-vampire, and a guy with a gun."

His ears perked up. "What guy? Why does he have a gun?"

"Allydia's great-great-whatever grandson. He's a detective."

"Oh," he said, his shoulders relaxing. "You mean Navid. I talked to him a little at the wedding. He seems okay."

"Yeah, I guess him and that Phindi girl are a thing now."

"Really? Huh. Well, that's--" Another clap of thunder shook the building so hard, a picture fell from the wall. Patrons jumped and choked on their drinks. Will peered out the window through sheets of rain. In the distance, standing in the middle of the river, he could see a figure, arms outstretched, palms facing the sky. "Hey, I need to call you back."

"Is everything okay?"

"I doubt it. Love you."

"Love you, too."

He ended the call and placed some money on the table. As he got up to leave, the room went dark. He turned back to the window and saw a wall of water come barreling toward it. "Look out!" he shouted, throwing himself at the waiter that had come to clear his table and shielding him as the glass shattered and a wave of river-water came rushing in. People screamed, running to the other side of the room as the building flooded.

"This way!" the manager called, opening the door to the kitchen and ushering customers through to the service entrance.

"Thanks, cutie," the waiter said, giving Will a wink before hurrying to the back.

When the room was cleared, Will headed to the front door, angrily mumbling to himself, "Lucifer."

"Hey!" Will shouted through the downpour. He stood on the edge of the river, his slacks and button-down soaked through. Behind him, cars drifted on the now flooded street. Streetlights were down, windows were broken. As he cupped his hands around his mouth to yell again, a stop sign flew by, carried by one hundred and fifty mile an hour winds, nearly taking his head off. He dodged it and bellowed, "Lucifer!"

The figure on the river turned and made its way to the shore, walking on top of the water as if it were pavement.

"It is you," Will said. "Of course, it is. What the hell are you doing?"

"What my Father commanded," Lucifer said. "You shouldn't be out here."

Will's phone buzzed in his pocket. He took it out, glanced at it, and put it back. "The Mayor's ordered a city-wide evacuation."

"Ah, well done, me, then." He smacked his nephew's back and pushed him toward the street. "Let's get you out of all this water before you drown and my brother has my head."

They trudged across to a building, Lucifer prying open the gate and breaking a window, shoving his hand inside and unlocking the door. They hurried in, their shoes half-submerged in the shallow water filling the room.

Will slammed the door shut, the wind outside no match for his inhuman strength. "I'm gonna need some information."

"My Father didn't tell you?"

He crossed his arms. "I didn't exactly give Him a chance. Why's He here? What the hell is going on?"

He leaned against the wall, taking a much-needed break. "It would seem a misguided witch released something she shouldn't have and now that the beast has been made flesh, he'll destroy this world and swallow the lot of you whole should my Father fail in His attempt to rescue you. I wouldn't worry too much if I were you, though. God isn't really one for failure."

"Right," he said, unconvinced. "Who's this monster?"

"His name is Moloch. He seeks power. He craves worship, feeds on it. The more souls that follow him, the stronger he becomes. Anyone unwilling to submit will be tortured and eliminated. Even his own minions are fair game for his whims. I once watched him flog a woman he called 'wife' for giving him a toothy--"

"Moloch, like child sacrifice and hellfire Moloch?"

"I see your education included religious studies. Very good. Yes, one and the same. In his true form, he's barely a threat but once corporeal he can gain worshipers and worshipers give him strength. Only my Father can defeat him and he will. He's done it before."

"How'd He do it before?"

He snickered. "He gave humanity a set of rules, most of which you all continue to ignore, the first being--"

"No gods before Him," he said, shaking his head. "So, He made people stop worshiping him."

"Yes. After some years, Moloch was rendered little more than a ghost. However, God has been wary of interfering in humanity's belief structures in the last few thousand years. I'm not sure what His plan is now."

"But, you're doing what He tells you, anyway?"

He tilted his head. "Of course. Have you forgotten who I am?" He stepped away from the wall, closing the space between them. "I will do as my Father commands. I need no context, no explanation. As long as He allows it, I will serve Him to the best of my ability. My advice to you is if you are asked to help in His efforts, you work as though the world depends on it because it probably does. Otherwise, stay out of His way."

Valerie ducked in the doorway, the rain coming down in sheets onto the roof of her sister's building. "Time for a break," she said, pulling her phone from her pocket and calling her husband.

"Hey, baby," he answered. "After a few meetings, I'm pretty sure we found our contractor. What have you been up to?"

"Angel shit," she told him. "Listen, I need you to go to your parents' in New Jersey."

"What for?"

"You see this storm, right?"

"Yeah, there's an evacuation order but--"

"But, nothing. Get out of town. I'll call you when it's safe to come back."

"You're not coming with me?"

She rested the tip of her sword on the floor of the stairwell. "This storm isn't Mother Nature, it's Lucifer."

"Lucifer? Why?"

"It is a long and fucked up story which I will tell you when I'm done with what I gotta do."

"What do you have to do?"

"I'm not sure yet. Fight someone or some thing. It's big." She looked out onto the pounding rain, her eyes falling as the nerves set in. "You know I love you, right?"

"Val, you're starting to scare me. Should I be worried? Because I am."

"I'm fine. I'll see you soon." She ended the call and shoved the phone back in her pocket. "I hope."

Chapter 23

Once safely at the house in Southport, Allydia retreated to the kitchen where she sat alone at the table desperately trying to get her anxiety under control. Navid and Phindi chatted on the sofa while Michelle paced the backyard, the early evening air like silk on her skin. The warm breeze did little to soothe her as she ended her call with Will. She went inside and sat at the table across from Allydia who took the opportunity to get out of her own head.

"Are you all right?"

"Nope," Michelle said, crossing her legs.

"How is your husband?"

"Freaked."

"And, his father?"

She dropped her phone onto the table. "You haven't talked to him?"

"I'm sure he's busy."

She leaned back in her chair, just noticing how concerned Allydia looked. "He loves you."

She nodded, her gaze distant.

"Are you...*insecure*?"

She tossed her hair over her shoulder and cleared her throat.

"You *are*."

She folded her arms and dropped her head.

"As much as seeing you squirm gives me joy, and it does, like, *a lot*, I have to tell you, I've seen how Will's dad looks at you. It's the same way Will looks at me. You're being crazy. That man loves you."

She lifted her chin, her eyes pooling with tears. "He's an angel and God has come calling. I am insignificant at best and at worst," She wiped away a tear that dripped to her cheek. "I was a *monster*. You don't know a quarter of the things I've done, the atrocities I've committed. I am irredeemable. God could demand he leave me or worse, restore his memories, make him Barachiel once more in which case he would flee from me of his own volition."

Her features softened as she leaned forward. "Listen, I don't know what God would do but my daughter would never ask anyone to give up someone they love, especially not her grandfather. She adores him. If there's even a smidge of her left in there, she won't ask him to."

"Elohim doesn't *ask*," Allydia retorted. "He forces your hand. He manipulates. If He wants us apart, He will make it happen."

Michelle pursed her lips and covered Allydia's hand with hers.

She looked at her with shock then gratitude, patting the back of her hand. "So, you forgive me, then, for kidnapping you?"

"Which time?" Michelle scoffed.

Allydia smiled. "Either?"

"I mean, I guess but only because you're sad."

In the living room, Navid went on and on about how amazing he thought it was that God was on Earth. "I wonder if I'll get to meet Him," he said, so excited by the idea that he didn't register Phindi's hand on his thigh.

"Do you not see how frightened the others are?" she asked. "He is the Creator, the one they call 'God Almighty'. Are you not afraid?"

"Not of *Him*. Maybe a little of whatever He's here fightin'. On the other hand, why should I be scared of that, either? If He's here, no chance that's posin' a problem for us, right?"

She looked him over, staring deep into his eyes which seemed to dance as they looked back at her.

He held her hand. "What?"

"You are strong, brave, and foolishly optimistic. If we survive the night, I will give you many children."

As the sun set over the city, residents scrambled to flee the flooded streets. Traffic backed up on bridges as car horns blared, the unrelenting rain making seeing to drive difficult.

A man slammed his fist into his steering wheel as he gritted his teeth, his wiper blades all but useless against the downpour. He rolled his window down and poked his head out, hoping to see the car in front of him inching forward. It didn't move. He honked again, waving to the other cars as he shouted, "Come on!"

He readjusted himself in his seat and had begun to put the window back up when he heard something strange in the distance. Over the pounding rain and car horns, another sound emerged. It was high-pitched, almost shrill but also guttural, like a wild animal dying alone in the woods. He looked through the windshield and in the mirrors but saw nothing but a gray wall of water. The noise got louder, its source drawing closer. Curious, he unbuckled his seat-belt and got out of the car.

The sky darkened as the shrieking persisted, so loud now that the bridge began to shake. The man put a hand over his eyes like a visor, desperate to see what could be making the horrific howl. After a few seconds, what looked like a shadow appeared above him. He squinted, unable to make it out.

Before he could think, the shadow rushed him, its mutilated face so terrifying, he couldn't even scream.

Chapter 24

Gabriel sat cross-legged on a log in the woods behind Poe's house as Wendy addressed Grace's coven, the angel's patience razor-thin as they had little time to get their ducks in a row.

The witches stood in a circle, holding hands and surrounding Wendy who concentrated on the faces of the women she saw in her mind's eye, hoping that she'd translated Lilith's teleportation spell properly. Tamsen had written it in Arabic and there was no way the others would be able to learn the spells in the time allotted if they were in a language most of them were unfamiliar with. Latin would have to do.

"Ad hunc locum," Wendy said, repeating the phrase once for every witch she meant to summon. One by one, they materialized inside the circle, the Priestesses of all the remaining major covens on Earth: From the United States, the Bassets, Bishops, and Leveaus. The Clarkes and Rigbeys from England and the Balfours from Scotland. From Italy, the Cantinis. The Nassars from Saudi Arabia and the Esus from Nigeria. From Ireland, the Meaths. From Australia, the Pauers. The Liangs from China, the Chantraines from France, and from New Zealand, Charlotte.

"Welcome," Wendy greeted as Grace's coven released their hands, allowing the women to spread out. "I apologize for bringing you here with no notice but we're pressed for time, so--"

"Why have you summoned us to this place?" the Leaveau Priestess snapped, pulling a curved blade from her belt and holding it in front of her.

Wendy sighed. "As I was saying, there's not a lot of time, so I'll get right to it. An old god called Moloch has come back to Earth. He's power-hungry, strong, and straight-up evil. Manhattan is under siege. If he's successful there, it's just a matter of time before he takes over the rest of the country and he won't stop with the US. The world is at risk. We need your help."

"Moloch?" the Nassar witch gasped. "But, how?"

"A shunned witch released him from Tituba's trap," Poe explained. "Now that he's corporeal--"

"A shunned witch?" the Leveau asked. "From *your* coven?"

"Yes."

She guffawed. "So, this is *your* responsibility. Why should we put ourselves at risk, *our sisters* at risk to clean up your mess?"

"That's valid," Wendy said. "But, and I hate to be that guy, who helped you when your dumbass sister let a fucking zombie loose in the French Quarter?"

The Leveau cleared her throat. "I appreciate that, Wendy. I do. But--"

"But, what?" Charlotte piped in. "You just don't believe in repaying debts?" She looked over the crowd, making sure to make eye contact with every witch there. "The island where I live would be underwater right now if not for this woman. I don't know what she's done for the rest of you but I'd venture to guess it's not nothing considering she's been our community's lifeline for the last what, fifteen years?" She moved to stand next to Wendy. "Millions of people would've died, including me, had she not saved our kiwi asses, so me and my girls will be there," She turned to face her. "Whatever you need."

"Wendy banished my daughter's abusive boyfriend," the Basset witch chimed. "She protected her. Count us in."

"Us, too," said the Bishop witch.

The Leveau Priestess put her hands on her hips after sliding the knife back between her belt and her dress. "I don't discount the Tituban's worthiness but this is *Moloch*. Have you all not heard the stories? The sacrifices of children? The torture? *He burned his enemies alive.*"

"Oh, for fuck's sake," Gabriel huffed, checking her phone and putting it back in her pocket as she stood. "We don't have time for this. Somebody kill me."

Wendy took a step back. "Huh?"

"I mean it, kill me. Now."

"Are you high?"

"Not since the 90s. I'm serious, let's go. Fucking kill me."

"No one's gonna *kill* you. What's wrong with you?"

"Fine, I'll do it myself." She waved a hand at the Leveau witch, freeing the knife from her belt and hurling it toward herself. It plunged into her chest, piercing her heart. She pulled it out and dropped it to the grass as blood spurted from her mouth.

Wendy screamed as a collective gasp sounded from the crowd. Blood poured from Gabriel's wound as her lifeless body fell, hitting the ground with a thud. Wendy covered her mouth, Poe catching her as her legs went weak.

A split-second later, the angel Gabriel exploded out of the body in a fiery glow. The energy-being had six wings and stood taller than the trees, its face indistinguishable from the rest of its incandescent body, a swirling inferno in the shape of a human. The angel lifted from the ground, hovering over the witches who huddled together, some curious, some terrified.

"I am Gabriel, Messenger of the Lord your God," a deep voice boomed from above. "A threat to all of humanity is eminent. Without your help, civilization as you know it will end. You have been summoned by the Almighty to do His work. The consequences of refusal will be swift and dire. Make your choice but be warned, if His efforts should fail, the blood of the innocent will be on your hands."

The figure of light shrunk down, disappearing into the corpse's chest. Wendy watched with tearful anticipation as the stunned crowd remained silent. Finally, Gabriel's eyes flew open as her hand jumped to her chest. She coughed as she took her first few breaths, Wendy kneeling beside her.

"Fuck me." She sat up. "Nope." She lay back down again, Wendy holding her hand. "That sucked *all* the balls."

"Are you okay?" Wendy asked, brushing the hair off her forehead.

"On a scale from meh to roadkill, I'm a solid shit factory."

"That's what you really look like?"

She took a few more deep breaths. "I don't really look like *anything*. That's just what people expect."

"We'll be there," the Meath Priestess called.

"Us, too," piped the Chantraine.

"And us," said the Esu.

The Liang witch nodded in agreement. "We are in, as well."

All the women nodded, all except the Leveau. She remained stiff, her expression stern as she retrieved her knife, wiping the blood from it on the grass.

Gabriel sat up and Wendy stood, taking a pile of papers from her bag and handing them out to the others. "Teach the spells to your covens and meet us at the designated time and place. Instructions are on the first page." She handed the Leveau Priestess a bundle of pages. "I appreciate all of your help. It won't be forgotten."

She gathered everyone inside the circle and made the command, "Reditu." The Priestesses disappeared, sent back to where they'd come from.

Grace's coven headed through the forest back to Poe's to practice the new spells while Gabriel leaned against the log, trying to get her bearings.

Poe joined Wendy a few feet away, eyes fixed on the exhausted angel. "You're girl, though!"

Wendy beamed. "*Right?*"

Chapter 25

Lucifer's face twisted in rage as he looked out the window.

"What?" Will asked.

He growled, flinging the door open and stepping out, waving his hand toward the sky, the rain instantly stopping, the clouds clearing.

Will followed him, the two standing knee-deep in water as Lucifer watched the skies.

"What are you looking at?" But as he followed his uncle's line of sight, he saw them, too, the thin, black wraith's streaking across the sky. There were thousands of them, descending into buildings and across the river.

"They're everywhere," Lucifer lamented.

"What the hell are those things?"

"Demons, let loose by Moloch, no doubt." He looked him up and down. "You nearly murdered me once."

"You want me to apologize again?"

"You're strong. Come with me."

"Where?"

He pulled him close, wrapping his arms around him and gripping him tightly as he struggled. "Hell."

"What?!"

They lifted off, springing from the flooded street and shooting into the night, Will kicking as they flew.

They touched down outside the abandoned power station, Will shoving away as soon as his feet hit the ground. "What the hell's wrong with you? You don't just fly people places without their consent."

"My apologies, William. I forgot my manners, time being scarce, you understand." He trudged into the building, Will following behind.

He coughed. "What is that?" He covered his nose with his shirt.

"Sulfur," Lucifer said as they moved through the building, the concrete floor becoming more and more cracked the closer they got to their destination. Finally, they came upon the crater, a gaping hole so deep, they couldn't see the bottom.

"Is that--"

"They've gone," Lucifer seethed, staring into the abyss.

"Who?"

"All of them. It's empty but for one. Only my sister remains. I can feel her, cowering, afraid to face our Father after everything she's done." He turned his back to the opening and began to leave. "Stay here. If Lilith steps foot out of this hole, use everything you've got."

"Everything I've got to what?"

He stormed out, angry determination coloring his voice as he answered, "Kill her."

"So, what should I call you?" Wyatt asked. "God? Elohim? Dad?"

"Sinclair's fine."

He arched an eyebrow.

"I'm still her, just also me. I know it's confusing."

"Truer words."

She pursed her lips, gazing out the window with furrowed brow.

"What's wrong?"

"The demons know I'm here. Moloch's mobilized them." She looked him in the eyes. "I know I've put you through it and you're not entirely happy with me right now."

He blinked, flashing her a contemptuous glare.

"I understand. But, I need you now, Barachiel. Are you with me?"

He leaned back and sighed. "Yeah, I'm with you."

"You're sure?"

"I haven't slept through an Apocalypse, yet. No reason to start with this one."

"Well, that's very good to hear because the demons have been set free and the people they're possessing need help. They can still be saved if we work quickly."

"What do you need me to do?"

"The witches will have to put their hands on them for the exorcisms. Once the demons have been removed, I need you to get those people to safety. Shock whoever you need to, but don't kill anyone. Those are innocent people, do you understand?"

He nodded, looking down at his hands folded on the counter.

"We won't be able to save them *all* but," She stopped, tilting her head, her features softening. "Hey,"

He met her gaze.

"You know how much I love you, right?"

"Are you speaking as Sinclair or God?"

"Yes."

He bit the inside of his cheek as tears threatened to form.

"One of the reasons I chose you to be here was because I needed to feel loved, too. Not devotion or fear. Not worship or admiration. Just real love from someone that didn't think I could do anything for them, that didn't expect me to be perfect or even helpful. Expectationless. Because of you, I've had that. Will, Michelle, Uriel, even Malik all love me more because I come from you. The traits I inherited from you through Will have endeared me to them. Your bravery and kindness, your unflinching honesty...your eyes. It wasn't Barachiel that gave me a family, it was Wyatt. *Wyatt* gave me true, unconditional love and I will always be grateful for that."

Tears spilled down his cheeks as she came around the island to hug him, rubbing his back and kissing the side of his head.

"I should tell you something else because I know you're curious." She wiped away his tears and brushed his hair away from his eyes. "Your parents aren't in Purgatory. They're together. They're happy."

He broke down, hugging her again and sobbing into her shoulder.

She placed a hand on the back of his head. "It's okay," she whispered. "I love you, Grandpa."

Chapter 26

Lucifer stormed down 7th Avenue, the floodwater clearing the pavement in front of him as he walked. He drove the river back to its rightful place, his face twisted in rage as his eyes fixed on the standoff happening in front of Times Tower. There they were, the demons that had escaped, every monster in Hell now occupying some poor human's body, lined up on the street, ready to do battle.

In front of them were seven witches whose power he could feel from fifty feet away. They'd clearly been advanced by the monster that stood front and center. Even in human form, Lucifer could see the wretched creature hiding beneath the surface, this thing that called himself a god.

Opposite the horde of evil stood his Father as the woman, Sinclair. The determination in her face gave Lucifer chills having seen the look more times than he could count. There was a time when he and God had battled side by side every century or so before The Almighty had decided to stop coddling humanity. Now, they'd fight together once more, the thought of it sending a shiver of excitement down his spine.

Wyatt stood on Sinclair's left with Valerie next to him as Lucifer took his place to her right. Behind them, Gabriel, Wendy, Poe, and her coven lined up, awaiting orders.

"Elohim," Moloch sneered.

"Tituba's bitch," she mocked in response.

Wyatt lifted his eyebrows, surprised by her language.

Moloch rolled his neck, ignoring the insult. "This world is mine, old man. You should start fresh somewhere else. I hear your precious humans are making great advancements in the colonization of Mars. Perhaps you could follow them there."

"Or, alternatively, you could make like a tree."

He tilted his head like a confused collie.

"*Leave.*"

He snorted. "Ah, I'd almost forgotten about your jokes. Funny, but you won't be laughing when I slaughter your children and the women foolhardy enough to follow you here. Seriously, you've come to stop me with *this*, a few angels and a handful of witches? All of Hell is at my back."

She leaned her head back. "Gabriel, what time is it?"

She checked her phone. "Nine on the dot." As she slid her phone back in her pocket, the other covens began to appear, teleporting in one by one. Thirteen covens materialized, one hundred and fifty-six women, all armed to the teeth with magic including Tituba's exorcism spell.

Poe furrowed her brow as she looked over the crowd. "The Leveau's aren't here."

"I see that," Wendy sighed. "Here's hoping we don't need them."

Across the divide, Blair placed a hand on Moloch's arm. "See the blonde with the better-than-everyone attitude?" She pointed in Wendy's direction.

He nodded.

"I want her to myself."

"So, have her." He took off his jacket and threw it to the ground, yanking off his tie as his body began to swell. Muscle tore through his clothes as he grew to twelve feet tall, his head doubling in size while massive horns sprouted from his elongated face. His skin glistened a muted shade of bronze in the moonlight, his head now that of a bull. His feet were replaced with hooves while his fingers formed razor-sharp claws. Steam wafted from his snout as gasps erupted from both camps.

Blair put her hand to her chest and licked her lips. "How are you sexier this way?"

He grunted down at her before turning his attention back to Sinclair, the low rumble of his voice booming in the still night air. "We were friends once, were we not, Elohim?"

She held her palms up at her sides, gathering energy. "No," she corrected. "You've always been a dick." She snapped her wrists forward, directing white-hot bolts of lightning into the beast's chest.

He stumbled back but corrected himself quickly as the energy dissipated. He lowered his head and let out a snarl before giving the order, "Attack!"

The demons charged, some wielding shards of obsidian and granite as swords, others without weapons relying on their superior strength to win the day.

Gabriel crouched in front of Sinclair, her hands held out as if to say 'stop', her telekinesis holding the horde at a distance while Sinclair shot bolt after bolt of lightning into Moloch's sizable torso.

Lucifer cracked his neck and winked at his brother. "Time to get to work." He bounded into the crowd, exorcising demons with one hand while fighting off more with the other. As the bodies of the unoccupied fell, Wyatt rushed to them, carrying them two at a time to the shelter of an abandoned fast-food restaurant several yards away.

The witches hurried to join the fight, shouting, "Ne transgrediaris!", immobilizing demons before reciting the exorcism spell. Wyatt scurried to help the freed humans to safety, throwing low-voltage balls of lightning at any demon that got in his way.

"What's happening?" a woman asked as he helped her sit in an empty booth. The others looked to him for answers.

"I don't know how to answer that," he told them. "Not without sounding like a lunatic."

"We were possessed, weren't we?" a young man asked, his hands shaking as he struggled to zip his hoodie.

Wyatt let out a sympathetic sigh.

"That's what happened to us, right?" the man asked. "That thing out there with the horns, that's the Devil, right? And, we were possessed by his demons?"

"Not exactly."

"What do you mean, 'not exactly'?" the woman snapped.

"We'll explain everything when this is all over. For now, stay here." He moved to leave but a man blocked his path.

"Who's 'we'?" he asked.

"I really don't have time for this."

"Make time."

Wyatt looked over the man's shoulder to see the battle unfolding in the street. Witches lay on the ground covered in blood while others were being beaten. "Get out of my way."

"Not until you tell us what--"

"People are getting killed!" he barked in the man's face. "I know you're scared but I don't have time to make you feel better right now. Move or I will move you."

The man's lip quivered as he stepped aside, the others in the building huddling together as Wyatt stormed out.

Back outside, he threw one bolt of lightning after another, clearing a path for the recently freed to race to safety. He came to the body of an older woman wearing a flower-print dress, a gaping head-wound pouring blood onto the wet pavement.

"Alice?" a woman yelped, crawling over and checking the body's neck for a pulse. "Oh, God, Alice!"

"Alice?" Wendy pointed the way for the man she'd just exorcised and came to kneel next to the corpse. She covered her mouth, tears forming in her eyes.

"Those monsters killed her," the grieving woman sobbed.

"I'm so sorry, Charlotte," Wendy said. "I shouldn't have let you come." She stood to address Wyatt. "Can you get them out of here, please?"

He nodded, patting her on the shoulder before picking up Alice's limp body. He escorted Charlotte and her coven to the restaurant, laying the dead witch in a booth, her sisters crying around her. The unpossessed looked on, tears of their own beginning to fall as panic turned to guilt for taking up their rescuer's time. Wyatt ignored their shameful glances and rushed back to where he was needed.

Wendy took her aggression out on the Gowdies, who now formed a barrier between Moloch and Sinclair's lightning. They deflected it, waving it away into buildings and billboards, rendering her ineffectual.

"Iikhmad," she growled, using Lilith's suppression spell to tamp down the witches' power as she stood before them.

"Absterben!" one of them shouted.

"Stirb jetzt!" another chimed in.

Wendy's jaw clenched as she stared them down, unable to control her anger. "Not tonight, bitches. Khudh alqua."

The Gowdies faces fell in horror as clouds of green light emanated from them and floated away, circling around Wendy before entering through her ears, nose, and mouth.

"What are you doing?" Gabriel asked as she fought to keep Moloch and the demons at bay.

"I took their power," she told her, stepping forward to face Blair who had been unaffected by Lilith's spells. "And, now I'll take yours."

The Gowdies ran, powerless and afraid as Blair's eyes went black. "You're no match for me anymore, Tituban."

She smirked. "Well, let's find out. Praefoco!"

She remained still.

"Subsisto!"

Nothing.

"Ignis!"

Blair rolled her onyx eyes and laughed. "As I said, no match. Herzbruch."

Wendy's hand flew to her chest as pain radiated from her heart down her left arm. She gasped for air as Blair laughed.

"Wendy!" Gabriel cried.

"Leave it alone," Sinclair instructed as she continued her assault on Moloch.

"She's dying!"

"I almost have him," she said through gritted teeth.

Moloch convulsed, barely keeping himself upright as electricity pumped through him.

Wendy fell to her knees, the color draining from her face as Gabriel pleaded.

"I have to help her."

Sinclair trembled as she increased the voltage. "Just…one…minute."

"She doesn't have a minute!"

Wendy collapsed onto the pavement, rolling her head to look into Gabriel's eyes. She whispered, "I'm sorry," before grabbing her hand. "Impartio."

Slowly, Wendy began to heal as Gabriel's abilities were shared with her. Gabriel watched, fascinated as Wendy waved her free hand in Blair's direction, engulfing her in a mushroom cloud of holy fire. The blast knocked the two sides apart, flinging Sinclair, Gabriel, and Wendy into the glowing, red staircase.

With Gabriel unconscious, Moloch and the remaining demons were free to move as they pleased. They marched toward the women while witches shouted out every spell they could think of to slow them down. Most were stopped in their tracks while Wyatt heaved lightning at the demons still moving. Valerie planted herself between the women and the horde, her sword igniting as she stood guard.

The women got to their feet as Moloch seethed. As his followers grew fewer in number, he became weaker. "No more games," he grunted, opening his mouth wide, releasing a black cloud of toxic gas.

Sulfur filled the air, choking the angels and witches. They coughed, their eyes watering. Wyatt pushed through, getting as many people to safety as he could. Soon, though, there were no freed humans left. The witches were suffocating, lying helpless on the ground as they struggled to breathe. Moloch approached the steps, the glint of victory in his eye.

"I've had just about enough of you," Lucifer said, getting between him and his sister. He flew into him, knocking the beast on his ass. He pried up the statue of Francis Duffy, breaking it free from its concrete pedestal.

Moloch stood, laughing, his hooves clonking as he stepped forward. "What are you planning on doing with that trinket?"

"What I always do...my damnedest." He swung the eight-foot-tall statue like a baseball bat, slamming it into the monster's face, the crack so loud, the crowd stood still. The beast's head turned, a few giant teeth falling from his smiling mouth. He laughed again.

Lucifer erupted with rage, hitting him over and over in the stomach and chest but his punches had no effect. Moloch remained unmoved, his maniacal laugh angering his opponent even more.

"Angels," Moloch mocked, wrapping his enormous hand around Lucifer's throat and lifting him off the ground. "Hardly worth the time it takes to snuff them out."

Lucifer kicked and punched but he couldn't break free from the beast's grip. Sinclair raced toward them but before she could reach them, Blair stepped in her path.

A sinister grin crept across the witch's lips, her ash-covered skin seeming to glow. "Geh weg." With that, Sinclair went flying into a billboard, smashing its orange lights, causing them to spark and blink out. She fell sixty-eight stories to the ground, her skull crushed on the sidewalk like overripe fruit.

Lucifer growled as he fought harder but it was no use. The beast had him.

Lucifer, he heard in his head. *Look at me.*

He couldn't move his head but he altered his glance to set eyes on his sister who held her throat, coughing as she sat up, keeping demons back with her mind. Tears sprung from her eyes as he listened to what she had to say. His eyes became saucers and he went ghost-white. She nodded and gave him a smile as he was consumed by Moloch's bright-white hellfire, dead so fast, he didn't have time to scream. The monster dropped his arm, nothing left of the angel he'd been holding but a cracked, charred cellphone that clinked on the pavement as Moloch brushed the dust from his hands.

He'd been so amused with himself, he hadn't heard the angel's brother screaming his name or the sound of his heavy footsteps as he bounded toward him.

Wyatt leaped on his back, grabbing the sides of his massive head and releasing every bit of energy he could muster. He took it from the air, the clouds, and the billboards. Electricity poured into the beast, causing his eyes to roll back and foam to sputter from his mouth.

Barachiel, stop! Gabriel begged.

I've got him.

You don't. Run!

But, it was too late. Moloch reached back with one clawed-hand and pulled Wyatt off, flinging him into the side of a building. He crashed through the wall and into an office space, his spine shattered on impact.

Gabriel looked to her sister standing next to her. *Don't do it.*

Valerie wiped the tears from her eyes. *Bitch, what the fuck do I have to lose?* She raced toward Moloch, sword raised. She plunged it in his gut, the wound combusting. But, as she pulled her weapon out of the monster's flesh, he bellowed a hearty laugh, the holy fire absorbing into his skin as if it were a welcome guest. He lifted his hand and swatted her away like a fly.

Poe crawled to Wendy on the steps. "We're getting slaughtered." She covered her nose and mouth with her shirt as she tried to breathe, coughing with every inhale. "There aren't many of us left."

The demons drew closer, Gabriel growing weaker by the second as the sulfur overtook her. She wouldn't be able to hold them off much longer.

Blair stood next to Moloch, both of them grinning as they waited for the angel to fall, leaving the door open for them to kill the rest of their enemies, including God.

"I don't know what to do," Wendy choked. "It's hopeless."

Gabriel's apartment sat empty, boxes of Wendy's clothes, books, and dishes left unopened in various rooms. It was dark, the only light still on being the UVA lamp over the lizard's terrarium. In her habitat, Pearl shuffled from one side to the other, her tiny heart beating a mile a minute. She rammed herself against the glass, Wendy's distress calling her like a beacon. She threw her pocket-sized body at the front of the terrarium, again and again, her tail thwapping against the glass with every strike. The noise echoed through the otherwise silent apartment. Had anyone been home, they would have been able to hear it all the way in the kitchen where the only other noise was the sound of the refrigerator's low hum.

After a few minutes, the noise from the habitat in the bedroom stopped. No more thwapping, no more shuffling. The apartment was quiet.

Moments later, another noise echoed from the bedroom, cutting through the air with sharp clarity. It was the sound of glass cracking.

Chapter 27

Wyatt came to in the dimly lit office, the sounds of the continuing battle several stories below coming in through the gaping hole in the wall. He tried to stand but barely got himself rolled to his back before the pain searing down his spine became overwhelming. He winced as his jaw tightened and his arms fell to his sides. He could feel his vertebra repairing themselves, the shards fusing together like jagged puzzle pieces. His legs were numb and his back was on fire. As desperate as he was to get back to the fight, he wasn't going anywhere until his spine healed. He looked up at the fluorescent lights, most of which were turned off for the day, and tried to come to terms with the fact that this might be his last night on Earth. He'd wanted to die so many times but not now. Now, he had things to live for, people that depended on him, people that loved him and that he loved. He couldn't let it end this way, not with that thing out there terrorizing the city. He had to survive this and if he couldn't, he at least had to take that monster down with him.

He grunted in agony as he took his phone from his pocket. The screen was cracked but it still worked. He found Will in the contacts and hit 'call'.

"Dad?" Will answered.

"Hey," he said, his voice scratchy. "Where are you? Are you okay?"

"I'm fine except Lucifer dragged me to the mouth of Hell to kill his sister if she tries to escape. Just another typical Tuesday night in this family."

Wyatt chuckled.

"Are *you* okay? You sound like you're in pain."

"Oh, I'll be fine in a few minutes but listen, if you don't hear from me again by morning--"

"Why wouldn't I hear from you?"

"*If* you don't hear from me, I want you to go to the house in Southport. It'll be safe there for a little while, at least."

"You're freaking me out, Dad. Are you saying there's a chance tha--"

"Promise you'll go."

"All right, I promise but how could Moloch win? Lucifer said--"

"Lucifer's dead."

"*What?*"

"Moloch incinerated him."

"Holy shit."

"I don't know what's gonna happen when I get back down there. I won't lie to you, it's not looking good. But, me and your aunts are gonna do everything we can. We always do."

"What about Sinclair?"

A tear rolled down the side of his face and into his ear as he remembered seeing his granddaughter's body fall and crash onto the pavement.

"Dad, where's Sinclair?!"

"I love you, Will."

"Dad!"

"Be good." He ended the call and wiped the tears from his face before calling Allydia.

"Wyatt, are you all right?" she answered, her voice frantic.

"For now." The pain in his back was starting to lessen and the feeling in his legs went from nonexistent to pins and needles. "You're safe?"

"Yes, we're fine."

"Good. So, I was wondering, if I'm still alive tomorrow, do you want to get married?"

She was silent for a moment.

"Allydia?"

"No."

"No?"

"No, tomorrow is much too soon. I'll need time to prepare, plan. Next spring?"

A relieved laugh tumbled from his lips as he smiled. "Whatever you want." He sat up, his spine fully mended. "I should get back."

"Of course. Wyatt,"

"Hmm?"

"Be careful."

He smiled again. "Love you, too." He ended the call and stood, his legs still shaky. He took a few wobbly steps to the opening in the wall and looked down at the battle below. He couldn't make out what was happening, he just knew it wasn't over, and as long as it wasn't over, there was still hope.

Wyatt limped from the building and through the sulfuric smog to find unoccupied humans scrambling to get away from the fighting. He guided them through the crowd, throwing balls of lightning at the demons that tried to stop him. He ushered the humans to the restaurant and turned back. There were a handful of witches still performing exorcisms but most had either been killed or were lying on the ground choking on toxic air. In the distance, he could see Wendy and a few more witches lying on the steps while Valerie swung her fiery sword, clanking it against the spears of rock some of the demons carried. She was fighting three at a time and even from afar, he could see she was exhausted.

Gabriel was on her knees, covering her nose and mouth with her shirt, still holding Moloch and the demons back. Wyatt let out a sigh of relief as he saw Sinclair walk up behind her.

"I can't keep doing this," Gabriel told her. "I can't breathe."

Poe was on the verge of passing out but as she lay there, coughing and eyes watering, her defeated expression altered. She beamed, smiling from ear to ear as she tapped Wendy's arm.

Wendy scrunched her brow and followed her friend's gaze. There, at the top of the staircase stood the Leveau coven.

Wendy rested her head back on the steps. "About fucking time."

The New Orleans witches took only a moment to assess the situation before their Priestess called out the first spell. "Evacuandam!"

"Evacuandam!" the coven repeated, their voices carrying over the crowd as though amplified by invisible loudspeakers. On their word, the cloud of sulfur dissipated, thinning out until it had completely disappeared.

Wendy, Poe, and the witches in the crowd caught their breath. Poe's coven remained intact while the rest had endured mass casualties. Their numbers had dwindled but they stayed on mission, exorcising as many demons as they could.

"It doesn't matter," Blair taunted. "The Leveaus are street performers compared to me. Poison air or not, you can't win."

Wendy offered her hand to the Leveau Priestess. "Take what you need." She took it, keeping her eyes fixed on the black-eyed witch as the rest of her coven joined her at the bottom of the steps. Poe held out her hand, too, the Priestess taking it in hers and gesturing to the coven to join hands, as well. They lined up, hand in hand as they awaited orders.

"Street performers?" the Priestess snapped. "We are not here for your entertainment, bitch." She glanced over to where Gabriel fought to hold Moloch off, noticing the woman standing behind her. There was a power radiating from her that she couldn't explain. It was breathtaking. She turned her attention back to Blair and said, "We're here to save the world. Conteram seorsum."

"Conteram seorsum!" the witches repeated.

Blair laughed. "You can't break me. You're weak. I'm," She looked down at her arms, dark lines spreading over their skin. "What the," The cuts grew deeper, blood seeping from them as she watched in terrified amazement. "What did you do?!"

"Conteram seorsum!" they shouted again, their voices echoing in the night.

Sweat beaded at Blair's temples as she started to hyperventilate, the cracks moving up her shoulders to her neck and face. She screamed as pieces of her fell to the ground, her body shattering like glass and crumbling to the pavement in a pile of wet flesh.

"Decrusto," the Priestess spat.

"Decrusto," the others repeated, the mounds of flesh and shards of bone disintegrating into blood and dust.

"Exteriores spatium."

"Exteriores spatium!" The muddy mixture lifted from the ground and floated up like a balloon, into the sky and out of the atmosphere.

The witches let go of one another. "You're late," Wendy said.

"Wasn't sure I was coming," the Priestess admitted.

"I'm glad you did."

She looked out over the crowd. "That's a lot of demons."

"Yep."

"Looks like we've got our work cut out for us. Come on, ladies."

They exchanged respectful nods as the Priestess led her coven into the battle.

Wendy's heart sank as she looked over to see Gabriel on her knees, hunched over with one hand up in front of her. Moloch was getting closer and she could see the exhaustion on her girlfriend's face. She wouldn't be able to hold him off much longer. She rushed to her, ducking to avoid the lightning Sinclair continued to pump into Moloch's chest.

"What do you need?" she asked. "How can I help?"

"I don't think you can," Gabriel told her, her voice strained.

"There's got to be something we can do," Poe said as she approached.

Gabriel thought for a second. "Help my brother. Get as many people out of there as you can...*fast*. There's only one way this ends."

The two nodded and bolted into the crowd, finding Wyatt and helping him take survivors to the makeshift shelter.

"There are too many," Gabriel told Sinclair. "I know you know I'm right."

"Just a few more minutes," she growled.

"I don't have any more minutes in me. I'm falling apart. I know you want to save these people but I can't keep them back any longer and if Moloch doesn't lose followers like, right the fuck now, he's gonna kill us all."

Sinclair remained determined, ignoring Gabriel and continuing her assault.

Gabriel's elbow hit the ground as she struggled to keep going, Moloch inching forward as she weakened. *I don't think I'm gonna make it,* she thought to Wyatt. *Moloch's closing in and he'll definitely squash me like a bug to get to Sinclair. Do me a favor.*

Of course, he thought back.

Gather the witches and people you've saved. Tell Wendy to use Lilith's teleportation spell to take you all somewhere else. Somewhere far.

You want us to leave? But, there are still thousands of--

There's no saving them. I have to use my last bit of energy to light their demon asses up.

She doesn't want those people to die.

I know. She's being stubborn, like always. God's way or the highway. But, we're out of time.

You're talking about defying God. Isn't that--

Yeah, He'll be uber pissed and I'll probably end up in a cage. I might even mope around all depressed and shit like Lucifer's been doing but I have no choice. It's kill a few thousand people or hand the planet over to this monster and a bunch of demons. We've tried it His way. It's time to use some common, human sense. Get those people out of there.

Gabriel,

Just fucking do it. She scanned the crowd to see Wyatt, Wendy, and Poe ushering a large group of people into the restaurant. *Is that all of them?*

Yeah, but--

Good. She set herself up and held out her free hand.

Gabriel, are you sure?

But, before she had time to answer, a strange noise blared in the distance, a shriek so shrill, it silenced the horde of demons trying to push through Gabriel's barrier.

What the hell was that? Wyatt asked.

I have no idea. Gabriel dropped her arm and looked around. "What is that?"

Sinclair stopped what she was doing and listened. "It can't be."

Another cry echoed in the dark, this time followed by the thunderous sound of massive, flapping wings.

Everyone looked up, including Wyatt who stood in the doorway of the restaurant, stunned by what he was seeing.

Another screech came from the animal as it drew closer and in the neon light of the billboards, everyone could finally see what it was: a black and white striped, thirty-foot dragon.

"Are you fucking kidding me?" Wyatt muttered as Wendy came out from inside to stand next to him. Their eyes were wide as their mouths hung open.

She knew as soon as she saw it but the word still came out as a question. "Pearl?"

Back on the steps, Gabriel glared at Sinclair who couldn't take her eyes off the creature. "Dragons are real?!"

Without altering her gaze, she answered by holding out her hand and tilting it from one side to the other.

The dragon shot down over the crowd of demons, opening its mouth to reveal rows of razor-sharp teeth. The demons tried to run but it was too late. From the back of Pearl's throat and out her open mouth, a wave of lava-hot fire erupted, burning demons to ash by the hundreds within seconds.

"Holy shit," Wyatt and Wendy whispered in unison as the dragon made a u-turn in the air and took another pass, incinerating hundreds more.

"You have a dragon?!" Poe asked, squeezing between them to get a better look.

"I have a *gecko*," Wendy said.

"You sure about that?"

Pearl flew over the crowd once more, setting hundreds more ablaze in one fell swoop. The remaining demons fled, abandoning the abomination they had once called 'savior'.

Gabriel's eyes rolled to the back of her head as she collapsed, fatigue overtaking her. Now unconscious, there was no longer anything keeping Sinclair and Moloch separated. With no followers left, however, Moloch was at a disadvantage. He was weaker but still self-assured. He rushed forward, his hooves splitting the concrete apart as they slammed down with every step.

"Fuck it," Wyatt said, racing toward the beast.

"What do you think you're doing?" Valerie asked, stepping in front of him.

He looked past her to see Sinclair's eyes go black, fangs descending as her arms stretched out to gather electricity from the air around her. He shrugged. "Helping?"

Valerie looked back, seeing the monster headed straight for her daughter. "Yeah, all right." Her sword again lit as the siblings ran toward them.

Sinclair pulled every bit of electricity from the surrounding billboards and buildings as she could, the air around her sizzling and snapping as lightbulbs and screens exploded, spraying glass and darkening the street. She let out a bellowing scream as she emptied the electricity into the monster's torso. He stepped back, grunting as he righted himself.

Wyatt, too, threw a steady stream of lightning at the beast, aiming at his head while Valerie crept up from behind. Moloch fell to his knees but kept coming, crawling on all fours, his shining eyes fixed on his enemy.

Gabriel awoke just in time to see Valerie raise her sword, its fire shining in beautiful, sunset hues against the blue and white bolts of lightning flooding into the monster's body.

Sinclair and Wyatt halted their electrocutions as Valerie plunged her blade into the beast's back, piercing his heart, and erupting out his chest. "Teach you to mess with *my* family, ugly ass cattle lookin' motherfucker." She pulled her weapon from his body, blood sputtering from his mouth, his eyes raised in surprise as he held a hand to the cauterized wound.

Gabriel sat herself up, waving a hand in Moloch's direction, this time her Holy Fire taking hold, engulfing him in flames. He screamed, his cries muffled by the fire. After a few moments, they stopped. He fell forward, his body turning to ash. As the flames died, so did he.

Valerie dropped her sword, its flame going out as it clinked on the cement.

"Everybody all right?" Wyatt asked.

Valerie nodded.

Gabriel struggled to stand. "More or less."

Sinclair wiped a tear from her eye, touching each of them on the arm before stepping over the smoldering pile of ash and walking onto the scorched battlefield.

"She'll get over it," Gabriel told them. "People dying just...isn't God's *favorite* thing."

Pearl flew over the street toward the restaurant, shrinking down to her original size and resting in Wendy's open palms. "You okay, pretty girl?" Wendy cooed as the gecko seemed to hiccup, a tiny puff of smoke escaping her smiling lizard lips.

Poe studied the animal, her eyes filled with wonder. "I knew familiars were as powerful as their witches but *my God*."

"What?" Sinclair called from a few yards away.

Poe froze. "Nothing, Ma'am. Sir. Ma'am. Your Holiness." She leaned in to whisper to Wendy. "She's God, right?"

Wendy nodded.

"Super weird."

"You're telling me. I babysat her once."

Gabriel joined Sinclair among the ashes of the dead. "Barachiel's gonna marry Dia. He's gonna be okay, I think."

Sinclair smiled. "I believe he will be."

"Not sure about Uri, to be honest."

She smiled again. "Don't worry about your sister. I've got her covered. As for you," She brushed a few stray hairs out of Gabriel's eyes. "You've done well. I'm very proud of you."

She nodded, tears welling in her eyes.

"Gabriel," She took her face in her hands. "You can rest now. Take a break. Live your life. Be Taran Murphy for a while. I won't call on you again. Well, not for a couple of hundred years, anyway."

Tears spilled down her cheeks and Sinclair wiped them away.

"You'll make them understand?"

She nodded as she sniffed back more tears.

"Thank you, Gabriel." She kissed her cheek and walked off, leaving the angel alone to cry in the dark.

Chapter 28

Shrieks of the damned pierced the night as their shadowy figures swirled around Will before diving into the chasm they'd clawed their way out of just hours before. Their wailing was so loud and the sight of them so ominous, Will had to cover his ears and flee his post, leaving the demolished gate to Hell unmonitored. He stumbled out of the building, ducking to avoid getting hit by one of the dark figures as it sped past. Thousands of the wraiths rushed in as Will hurried to escape them, tripping in the gravel and falling on his rear. He sat there, ears covered, watching as they filtered in. After a few moments, they were gone, their shrill cries replaced by welcome silence. He dropped his hands, letting out a sigh of relief as he saw Sinclair approaching from his left.

"Is it over?" he asked.

"Almost," she said, offering a hand to help him up.

He took it and stood. "My dad?"

"He's fine. Your aunts and Wendy, too."

His shoulders relaxed as he let out a breath.

"I have to go now."

He nodded. "Will Sinclair remember being...you?"

Her eyes softened and she tilted her head, touching his cheek before hugging her arms. "No, she won't. Listen, Hell's gate isn't open, it's broken, decimated. In this body, I can't just blink it fixed. It requires a spell...and a sacrifice."

His jaw tightened. "What kind of sacrifice?"

"Blood, for starters, of someone from our line. Your father's line. Sinclair blood. Did you read The Da Vinci Code?"

He shook his head. "How much?"

She bit the inside of her cheek. "Just...all of it."

"No."

"Mine, not yours."

"Out of the question."

"Well, if that's upsetting you, I don't even want to tell you the second part."

"Second part?"

"To seal the gate completely, the spell requires another ingredient." She put her hand to her chest. "The heart of the divine."

He took a step back as the color drained from his face.

"Please stop freaking out. It's okay."

"*Okay*?!"

"If the gate isn't sealed now, the demons that just got sucked back into Hell will climb right back out, not to mention the thousands that are still out there."

"No. You might be God but you're in my daughter. I forbid it."

"You what?"

"I forbid it. You're not killing my daughter. Figure something else out."

"Sinclair has known who she was since the moment she was born. She always knew it would end this way. She understands why it's necessary. You should, too."

"I said '*no*'." He formed a ball of lightning in his hand and threw it at her, hitting her in the stomach and knocking her to the ground.

She looked up at him in annoyed confusion. "Really?"

He shocked her again, this time with more voltage.

"Are you serious?" She got to her feet. "I'm God."

He threw a bolt of lightning hard into her chest, its force sending her reeling back and into the gravel. He stood over her, another orb of energy forming in his palm. "Fuck God."

She scurried out of the way just as he threw the ball down, narrowly avoiding a shock to the face. She raced around to the other side of the building and back in a blur, now carrying a heavy, rusted chain. "I won't fight you but you won't stop me." She used her hyper-speed to rush him, wrapping him in the chain from neck to ankle.

He struggled against the iron as she closed the space between them.

"When you and Michelle are ready, Sinclair's human soul will be back. Maybe she'll be a boy next time. Do you have a preference?"

He shook his head, tears pooling in his eyes. "Please, don't do this."

"What kind of God would I be if I let my Creation be destroyed? There are thousands of demons out there and thousands more beneath our feet. How many people do you think they'll kill? What kind of pain they'll cause? What unimaginable torture will they inflict? I have to do this. Hey," She lifted his chin as tears slid down his cheeks. "You'll be okay. You all will be. I made sure." She wiped away his tears and kissed his cheek before pushing him to the ground. He winced as his chained back slammed into the gravel and concrete. "Stay here. When you make your way out of that, go home. Stay out of this building. You shouldn't see any part of this."

"Stop!" he cried as she entered the decrepit building. "Wait, please! Stop!"

She ignored him, taking one determined step after another toward the dark fissure. Once upon it, she sat down, legs dangling over the edge into the void. She let her fangs grow, holding her left wrist to her quivering lips. With her pointed teeth, she tore open the artery, cringing as she held her arm out over the chasm, letting the blood drain.

She took a deep breath and began the spell. "Ghalq hadha bawwaba." Inside, the walls started to close in, rock and earth fusing to fill in the deepest parts of the breach. She pulled her legs up and sat on her knees, whispering to herself, "This is gonna suck." She took another breath before starting again. "'Aydaan," She put her fingertips to her chest and sank them in, penetrating the muscle and breaking through bone. "Aihtafaz," she grunted as she wrapped her fingers around her fast-beating heart. "Mugfal." Her whole body shook as she ripped the heart from her chest, dropping it into the chasm. As her eyes rolled back, her face falling and her muscles going limp, the shards of Hell's gate came together, the mass of vacancy fully repaired.

Outside, the ground vibrated with the sound of thousands of demons fast approaching. They howled as they were pulled out of the bodies they'd been occupying, through the air, over Will, and into the building.

"No!" he shouted, fighting harder to get free of his chains. "Sinclair!" It took less than a minute for all the remaining demons to be hauled back to their rightful place, the gate's lock now secure. In the quiet of his solitude, Will sobbed, his arms aching against the iron that bound him. Finally, one link broke, snapping apart and clinking on the rocky ground. Another link cracked, then another. Soon, enough of the chain had been broken that he could move his arms and wiggle himself free.

He raced inside, dismissing Sinclair's instructions to go straight home. He tore through the building back to where Lucifer had left him. There, he found her, her hands and arms covered in blood, a gaping wound where her heart used to be. "No," he whimpered, kneeling next to her and gathering her in his arms, holding her the way his father had once held him, tears pouring down his face as he brushed the hair away from his daughter's empty eyes. He rocked her, kissing her head and weeping, his heart completely broken.

Chapter 29

"They'll be all right?" Wyatt asked as the spared humans filed out of the restaurant, their dead stares having him question the witches' decision to spell them.

"They'll be fine," Wendy told him. "They'll go home, go to bed, and wake up tomorrow like nothing happened. They won't remember a thing."

"Are you all right? I know you lost a lot of friends tonight."

She let out a breath, holding back tears as she pet Pearl's head. "I did." She looked up at him with a sympathetic smile. "But, you lost a brother."

He dropped his head and chewed on his lip.

"Go be with your family. I'll finish up here, give you a few minutes before I come over and do the supportive girlfriend thing." She turned her gaze to Gabriel who still stood on the battlefield. "Maybe I'll make her a cake. Or brownies. Or cookies? There's an oatmeal butterscotch recipe I've been wanting to try."

"I'd go with all three."

They both laughed. "Okay. All three it is. And, I'll bring some by your place, too."

"Thank you."

She nodded as he touched her arm and walked away.

Valerie sat on the steps, their red light flickering as she rested. Her phone buzzed in her pocket and she answered it, happy to see Malik's number lighting up the screen.

"Hey, I was just about to call you."

"So, it's over?" he asked, hope in his voice.

"Yeah. It's definitely over."

"And, you're okay?"

"As okay as I can be, I guess. Gabriel says we're done with our angel shit. No more visions, no more monsters."

"Are you serious?"

"That's what the girl said."

"I am real glad to hear that because I just got a call from the adoption agency."

"Now? It's the middle of the night."

"Someone chose us."

She sprang up. "What?"

"She's in labor right now in Albany. I'm already in the car on my way."

Her stomach flipped as tears of joy welled in her eyes. "Text me the hospital's address. I'll meet you there." She ended the call and darted off, blowing by Wyatt as he walked over to meet Gabriel.

God's Messenger crouched down to pick up what was left of Lucifer's cellphone, now little more than a lump of charcoal. She held it to her chest as her brother knelt next to her.

"You okay?" he asked.

"Not really." She fiddled with the phone, pieces of it breaking off in her hands. "It's been a day."

He nodded in agreement.

"It's gonna be weird not having him around, making snide comments, criticizing my eating habits."

"Well, if you want, I can pick up the slack in that department. You do eat way too much sugar."

She laughed. "Almost. Next time, try it with a little more flair."

He chuckled. "I'll work on it. Maybe I'll fake a British accent."

"I'd appreciate that," she giggled, fresh tears falling from her puffy, red eyes.

Wyatt ran a finger over the phone, tears of his own threatening to spill. "I'm gonna miss him."

"You'll see him again."

He blinked, raising his eyebrows. "I'm going to Hell?"

She wiped away her tears and looked up at him, a soft laugh escaping her upturned lips. "No."

Lucifer floated through Heaven's great halls, nostalgia washing over him as he was enveloped in the warmth of pure light. Wandering past the levels in which human souls resided, he made his way to the angelic realm. Once there, he quickly bypassed the Cherubim, finding himself where his existence had begun, in the Choir of the Seraphim.

"Lucifer," he heard a voice call.

"Yes," he responded, recognizing it immediately.

Before him materialized the figure of a man with bright blue eyes and five-o'clock shadow. This must have been the appearance of the human he'd been born into nearly forty years prior.

"Camael. It's good to see you. I was sorry to have missed you on Earth."

"That's all right. That version of me would have found you obnoxious."

He laughed. "You're probably right."

"It's good to see you, too. Gabriel told me to look out for you when you got here. Said you'd need time to adjust."

"She did, did she? Why am I not surprised? Always feeling the need to control things, that one."

"She just loves you. We all do. You're going to have to get used to feeling that again."

"You're here!" another voice called. Forming in the ether was the image of the man that had called himself Tae.

"I am. It's nice to see you again, Raphael."

"How is my niece? Did she get into the university she wanted?"

Lucifer held back a snicker. "We'll talk later."

"Brother!" Michael cheered, manifesting before him in a glittery haze. He appeared as a tall man with dark, shoulder-length curls and golden-brown eyes. "It's been too long."

"Agreed."

Michael hugged his brother and patted him on the back. "I've missed you."

"Likewise."

"Tell me, what is Hell like?"

"Perhaps a story for another time."

"Of course. I'll admit, when Father told us you'd be back, I was almost afflicted with emotion."

He chuckled. "I'd recommend avoiding it. Wouldn't want to hurt yourself."

"He's still asleep but He said He'll see you as soon as He wakes."

Lucifer looked to the gleaming set of doors a few feet away, the low vibration of his Father's energy emanating from just beyond them. He moved to stand in front of them, placing a hand on the smooth surface. "I'll just wait here, then."

"For two hundred years?" Michael asked.

"Getting even the smallest of glimpses of Him on Earth was enough to remind me of how much I needed Him. I've endured the ache of Separation for thousands of years. Two hundred will go by like minutes."

He stood next to him and put his arm around his shoulders. "If that's what you want, I'll wait with you."

Lucifer smiled, staring eagerly at the doors, the happiest he'd ever been.

The End

The Complete Seventh Day Series

Seraphim
Nephilim
Elohim
Cain
Alukah
Coven
Sinclair

Made in the USA
Coppell, TX
05 May 2025